BOOKS BY K.W. CALLAHAN

THE SYSTEMIC SERIES: DOWNFALL

THE SYSTEMIC SERIES: QUEST

THE SYSTEMIC SERIES: DESCENT

THE SYSTEMIC SERIES: FORSAKEN

THE SYSTEMIC SERIES: ASCENSION

AFTERMATH: PART I

AFTERMATH: PART II

AFTERMATH: PART III

THE M.O.D. FILES: THE CASE OF THE GUEST WHO
STAYED OVER

THE M.O.D. FILES: THE CASE OF THE LINEN
PRESSED GUEST

PALOS HEIGHTS

PANDEMIC DIARY: SHELTER IN PLACE

PANDEMIC DIARY: FLEE ON FOOT

PANDEMIC DIARY: PANDEMIC PIONEERS

K.W. CALLAHAN

PANDEMIC DIARY: SHELTER IN PLACE

Text and image copyright © 2016 KW Callahan

Callahan, K.W.
Pandemic Diary: Shelter in Place / K.W. Callahan

ISBN: 1-523-88893-8

PANDEMIC DIARY: SHELTER IN PLACE

Friday, August 30th

6:18 pm

I've never kept a journal before, but after today, I decided this might be a good time to start. I wanted a way to document what I've seen happening lately. I don't really want to talk to Kate about it. I don't want to scare her. But I need some sort of outlet to get this stuff off my chest. I mean, today at work is a perfect example. People were going ape shit over nothing. They're all whacked out about this flu thing that's supposedly going around. Sure, I don't exactly want to get sick either, but hell, I got my flu shot. And while I know that's no guarantee I won't pick up a new strain, it's not like I'm in the demographics for dying from the flu. That's what happens to old folks and babies, right? They're the ones most commonly killed by the flu…at least that's what I've heard. Still, people are going a little bit nuts.

Anyway, back to my wild day at work. So I get there at about quarter of seven, just like usual. I get my coffee, check my voicemail, read emails, run the daily assignment sheets, get them handed out right on time at eight, do the morning meeting, and everything is going smooth. Just a normal Friday. After the morning meeting, I head back to my desk, flip on the television in my office, and start to respond to a few of my email messages. The news was on, and a reporter downtown was interviewing people about this flu that's going around – the "Su" flu they're calling it since they say it originated in the Gansu province of China.

So the news guy is talking to a middle-aged black woman about whether she was taking any extra preparations to avoid the flu this year. There's a crowd of people around her and suddenly one of them starts coughing. It wasn't any big deal, just some dude coughing, like he's got something stuck in his throat. But this big guy next to him starts yelling and then shoves the coughing guy away. He's going nuts because he thinks the coughing guy might have the flu and is spreading it around. The guy he shoves doesn't care too much for being pushed, and he pushes the bigger dude right back. Anyway, it all breaks down. The two guys start fighting right there on the street on live television. Then a couple more people get involved trying to break up the first two and it becomes an all-out free-for-all. It was pretty awesome, but I'll admit, at the same time it was kind of scary. It shows just how far people will go if they feel threatened.

Amazingly, that wasn't the craziest part of the day. After lunch, Jessica, one of my favorite sales people from a local supplier, stopped by the office. She usually pops in every other week or so just to check in, kill a few minutes chatting and take our regular order. It's not necessary, just a nice customer service tactic in what seems to be an increasingly impersonal business world…but I digress.

So Jessica rolls into my office just after lunch time. We chat for a few minutes, and she tells me she's picked up a late-summer cold – likely from one of her kids who started school last week. We're just shooting the breeze, talking about our kids, our plans for the weekend, stuff like that. Then, while I'm giving her our supply order, two of our building's security guards come into the office; they don't even knock, they just barge right in. Being a small manufacturing facility that operates out of one half of the building, there's not a large security force around. It's usually just a couple guys who monitor the parking lot and do a roaming patrol of the building and exterior grounds. So it was a surprise for them to come into my office. Weirder yet, they were wearing white masks (like doctors in surgery wear) and latex gloves.

I asked them what was up, but they just ignored me. Instead, they headed straight for Jessica. She was in the middle of blowing her nose when they grabbed her kind of roughly and hauled her out of the office. I didn't have a clue as to what was going on. I thought maybe she'd done something wrong; you know, run over somebody in the parking lot or stole something. My mind was running wild with what might have elicited such a response from the guards. I tried to get them to stop, but they just kept kind of pushing and pulling Jessica along between them. They totally ignored me. In fact, I took a pretty good elbow to the midsection when I got in the way at one point when they were hauling her outside.

6

I felt bad for her. She didn't appear to know what the hell was going on either and was completely freaking out. She started yelling about lawsuits and everything else. I couldn't blame her, it was nuts!

Seeing Jessica coughing and blowing her nose, I guess somebody from our office had called security. Thinking she had the flu or Su flu or whatever, they reported her to security. In turn, security – having been watching all the news coverage of this new flu strain – was hyper-sensitive to anyone they thought might have it. So they must have called the authorities. In turn, the police must have sent a response team to the building, which according to the nightly news, I guess is the new norm for handling this kind of thing.

So they ended up hauling off poor Jessica. I followed her outside where there were two police cars and a mobile unit from the CDC waiting. I haven't heard from her since. I called her a couple times on her cell, texted her, emailed her, and even called her office. They haven't heard from her either.

It's wild. Almost like a movie. I asked around after Jessica was taken away, but nobody owned up to calling security. I have a feeling it was my assistant, Jerry. I noticed him on the phone a few minutes after Jessica arrived, but he denied it.

By the end of the day, two employees who had exhibited cold or flu-like symptoms had been sent home, two more had been hauled off by the CDC, and five more were refusing to come to work next Tuesday after the long weekend. Out of the 15 employees in our office, only six were willing to return to work after Labor Day, and most of them only agreed to do so on the condition that this flu thing settles down over the weekend. With a potential walkout on my hands, I gave Suzanne (our regional VP) a call. She said to call it an early weekend and shut the office down for the rest of the day. About 30 minutes ago, I got a text from her telling me that we are keeping the office closed until further notice due to the spreading flu virus.

Well, that's enough for now – my hand hurts. I'm not used to writing this much anymore. Reminds me of grade school. Plus, it sounds like Violet and Dylan are fighting and Kate's having a tough time wrangling the little beasts to sit down for dinner.

Guess it's time for Superdad to save the day (yeah…right!).

10:48 p.m.

Yes, I'm still awake, writing in near darkness. I can't sleep. Kate's here in bed beside me, out like a light...as usual. That girl could sleep through nuclear Armageddon.

I've been flipping back and forth watching the non-stop television coverage of this Su flu stuff on all the news networks. It's kind of cool but kind of frightening at the same time. With work and all, I haven't paid much attention to it lately, but I guess this new flu strain is more serious than everybody thought, or at least more serious than *I* thought.

Sure, I've been seeing the headlines in the newspapers and "alerts" on the news. But to be honest, I just figured it was the usual attention grabbers to gain readership or get more viewers while distracting us all from how terribly the politicians are doing their jobs. Now it looks like some people have actually died from this flu strain, and not just *old* people, people my age, and Kate's age – healthy, reasonably young people.

It seems as though people are starting to get nervous about all this. The current flu vaccine doesn't seem to be working and they have no backups or alternatives to combat the spread of this strain. The symptoms sound pretty terrible. I guess the virus ends up shutting down vital organs, and it happens pretty quickly.

I'm worried about work too. I don't want the office closed for too long. If we're down for more than a week, it's going to kill our numbers for the quarter and that could mean missing the mark for our annual bonuses. That would suck big time. No vacation to Florida for the holidays if that happens. The kids would be SUPER disappointed.

Okay, time to try to get some sleep. I doubt things will change much between now and when Violet comes sneaking into our bed at the ass-crack of dawn.

P.S. – A note for tomorrow: Make sure to go with Kate to the store in the morning. Load up on some extra water, canned goods, cereal, milk, etc. I don't want to sound like a nut, but after watching all these news reports, I'm starting to get nervous.

Saturday, August 31st

7:32 a.m.

Well, I was wrong. Things HAVE actually gotten worse since last night.

According to the local news, Chicago area hospitals continue to see an influx of flu-related patients. City emergency services are being stretched to the limit by calls from people who think they might be sick but are afraid to go to the hospital. They think that if they don't already have the flu, by going to the hospital, they might catch it there. Then there are the people who would like to go to the hospital but are afraid to because to get there, they'd have to take public transportation, which city officials are saying is a Petri dish for flu breeding. I guess this thing is EXTREMELY contagious so people are being advised to stay home unless it's absolutely necessary to leave.

If you're dying from the flu, though, isn't it kind of necessary to leave?

Meanwhile, I get the weekend shopping duties. Yea me!☹ The whole family was supposed to go together, but with all this flu talk, I decided it would be safer for me to go alone. I want to stock up on some extra stuff anyway...just in case.

11:48 a.m.

Well that whole experience was INSANELY ridiculous. It took me almost four hours to get to the grocery store (only a mile away), get some of what we needed, and get home. The streets were jammed. The parking lots were packed. The store was filled to capacity. I guess I'm not the only one with some concerns about this flu thing. Thank God we don't live closer to downtown. I can only imagine what a mess it is there.

9

I was only able to get about half of what was on my list. Kate and the kids are currently working on putting the stuff away. Sweet Violet digs stuff out of the bags, hands them to Dylan, who in turn gives them to Kate. It's the cutest little assembly line.

While they finish up, I'm going to take the opportunity to walk over to Devries', a locally-owned grocery store just a couple blocks from our condo. Because they're a neighborhood market, they tend to have higher prices and a smaller selection of products, thus the reason we don't typically shop there. It also means that they aren't usually as busy as the big chain stores. Hopefully, I can find the rest of what's on my list there.

1:13 p.m.

Back from Devries'. It was pretty crowded but not as bad as the big grocery store. Cost me an arm and a leg, but I got corned beef, powdered milk, and some stuff that the other store was out of. The shelves at Devries' were already looking pretty bare. I'm glad I was able to get out fairly early and load up when I could. Now we can settle in and enjoy the rest of the long weekend.

9:03 p.m.

Just a few thoughts while Kate gets Dylan tucked in and before we watch the movie we picked up from the library the other day.

First, this flu thing might really be something serious. I'd like to go to Riverside tomorrow for the picnic we'd planned, but I'm not sure it's the best idea. I think that maybe we should just stick around the house this weekend. I don't want to be a reclusive shut-in or anything, but I also don't want to risk anyone getting sick.

Uh oh, Kate's back now, movie in hand. She's giving me the evil eye. We don't get much alone time anymore. I'd better stop writing before she falls asleep on the couch and we have to postpone movie night...again. It'd be the third time this month.

10

Sunday, September 1st

4:38 p.m.

We just got back from Riverside a little bit ago. I know I said we were debating whether or not to go, but I'm so glad we gave it a whirl.

It was a hot, yet lovely day. It was only around 80 degrees, but the humidity made it feel more like 90. There wasn't a cloud in the sky, and a soft breeze at least helped to circulate the moist air.

We parked near the library and took a brief walk around Fredrick Law Olmstead's incredibly well-planned community. We love to absorb the classic beauty of the village's massive Victorian homes. After that, we walked down to the park that borders the Des Plaines River. There, Dylan and I threw the football for a bit while Kate and Violet picked flowers, chased butterflies, and inspected various beetles and other bugs. Then we regrouped and spent a few minutes throwing rocks into the river. I used the opportunity to teach Dylan how to skip some of the flatter rocks we found along the river bank over the water's surface. He got a couple successful skips in before we continued walking along the path that follows the river to nearby Lyons, where the big dam used to be. But we didn't want to walk too far since Violet was hungry and complaining that her feet hurt.

So we made our way back to the car, unloaded our picnic basket, and ate lunch in the park between the library and the historic train station. From our spot, we were able to watch the Metra trains shoot back and forth between downtown and the western suburbs as well as a couple freight trains or "freighters" as Violet calls them, rumble past.

Kate had packed ham sandwiches for us, and we gorged on potato chips, chocolate chip cookies, some potato salad, juice boxes for the kids, and bottled waters for me and Kate.

All in all, it was a wonderful day. Better yet, no one was really around, so we had very little contact with the public, thus, no worries regarding the flu.

** Mental note: Violet loved playing at the park. Doing something in Riverside might be a good idea for her 5th birthday coming up next month.

Monday, September 2nd
(Labor Day)

9:13 a.m.

Well that wasn't fun. I just finished breaking the bad news to the kids that we won't be attending the Labor Day baseball game between the Cubs and Sox. Dylan took it the hardest. The tickets were his 8th birthday present several months ago. Now both kids are in their rooms crying.

For as nice as yesterday was, today is starting off pretty shitty. Heck, I'm disappointed myself. I'd been looking forward to the game for months, and I hate playing the bad guy and disappointing the kids. But after watching the news this morning, there was no way I was going to take my family downtown on the train to sit among a human stew of bacteria at the ballpark. If anyone wants to get sick, that would be the way to do it in my opinion.

Apparently, things aren't getting any better out there with this flu thing. In fact, it looks like they're getting worse. A lot of events are being cancelled for tomorrow, numerous businesses are saying they'll be closed, and Kate and I are wondering whether Dylan will have school.

There have been more deaths from the flu and the hospitals are still jammed. I don't like the way this thing is headed. There still hasn't been any report of available vaccines, and it looks like Chicago isn't the only big city having problems with this particular flu strain. In fact, just about every major city is reporting widespread outbreaks and massive influxes of patients at their hospitals…and dozens of deaths so far. News reports are currently estimating flu-related deaths are already topping 1000 nationwide – kind of freaky stuff if you ask me. Worse yet, it seems that once you get the virus, it only takes a couple days for it to kill you. It spreads from organ to organ, shutting them down, leaving the

13

host's body unable to mount any sort of defense against the disease. Sounds pretty terrible. I think the scariest part is that from the reports I've heard, no one is getting better after coming down with the virus.

Not good…not good at all.

2:28 p.m.

It's been a pretty crummy Labor Day so far. Everybody is still upset about having to miss the baseball game. I'm watching it on television by myself. Violet is down for her nap. Dylan is playing video games in his room, and Kate is reading in our room. She said she'd make everybody's favorite for dinner tonight – tacos – in an attempt to perk us up. It's days like today that I wish we had a house with a yard. I mean, I love condo life for the security and the ease of lifestyle it provides – not having to rake leaves, cut the grass, constantly make home repairs, that kind of stuff – but I miss being able to just pop outside, throw the Frisbee, play ball with the kids or just get some fresh air. If property taxes weren't so damn high here, it'd be a consideration, but paying ten grand a year or more just for the honor of owning the property itself seems ridiculous to me. I don't know how some of these people do it. Of course a lot of them are dual-income families. But if Kate was working (besides doing her internet stuff that is), we'd have to pay for daycare for Violet and an after-school program for Dylan, and that would be another huge chunk of change. Oh well, condo life isn't all that bad; I just miss having a yard is all.

6:28 p.m.

Dylan's bouncing off the walls with excitement. We just got a phone call from his school with a recorded message from the district superintendent telling us that classes are cancelled for the entire week. I'm glad they called because Kate and I were having a tough time deciding what to do. We were going to let Dylan take the day off tomorrow anyway, just to be on the safe side, but we weren't sure what to do after that. We really didn't want to let him go back with the flu spreading like crazy, but we also didn't want him missing too much school.

Well, problem solved. But I'm somewhat concerned about how long all this is going to last. It could really screw up his summer break. I know that Kate had activities planned for Dylan starting the second week of June. If his school gets extended much longer due to the flu outbreak or because of snow days later this winter, it could have Kate scrambling to try and reorganize his summer schedule.

Well, at this point, I guess we'll cross that bridge when we get to it. For now, the boy is pumped up about no school. I DID inform him however that it won't be all video games and TV watching, and that he has to read and do some math practice too. That kind of tempered his excitement…but not much.

9:28 p.m.

This won't be a long entry since I'm getting ready to go to bed. I think that just sitting around the house actually makes me feel more tired than when I'm out doing stuff…even working.

Really, I just wanted to do a quick Su flu update. Television coverage of the flu is nearly nonstop now. Hospitals are filled and overfilled. Apparently hundreds of people are dead or dying and they don't have room for the bodies. It's all pretty horrible. I've decided that tomorrow I'm going to make one more run to Devries' grocery store to see if there is anything left. I'd like to stock up on a few more items just to be on the safe side and then hunker down for a while. After this trip, I really don't want to go into public places any more than I have to for the rest of the week. By then, they'll hopefully start getting this thing under control.

Tuesday, September 3rd

6:57 a.m.

I'm writing early this morning because I want to get a jump on going to Devries'. I'm hoping I can beat the rush, get there while they still have some stuff available, and avoid as many people as possible.

I'm wearing a white surgical-style mask that I picked up this weekend at the store (I think it's more for home repair work than preventing disease, but it's all they had). And even though it's just a couple blocks, I'm going to drive so that I can get more stuff. Dylan's pestering me to come. He's going stir crazy having been shut up in the condo all day yesterday, but I'm not letting him. He went back to bed in a huff. Just as well. Letting him sleep is the best way to keep him out of our hair. I don't know what we're going to do with him being home all week. I know he's excited about not having school and thinks this is all some sort of extended snow day, but I'm afraid he's quickly going to get tired of sitting around inside. But I'm definitely NOT letting him out around other people.

I don't really have a shopping list for this trip. I'm just going to see what's left and try not to be too picky. If we like it, if it's got a reasonable shelf life, if it's available, and if it's not too expensive, I'm probably going to buy it. I don't see any reason to chance it at this point. It's not like we won't eat the stuff eventually, especially the way Dylan has been going through food lately. I swear that kid hits a growth spurt every other week. He's going to be as tall as his mother soon.

Okay, better get moving. Devries' opens at 7 a.m. and I want to be there when the doors open.

10:23 a.m.

There was a line almost 20 deep when I got to Devries'. A lot of people were wearing masks similar to mine. It reminded me of photos I'd seen of airports or bustling city streets in Asia during the bird flu, SARS or similar outbreaks. A couple people, apparently unable to come up with masks, were wearing scarves over their faces. It's strange to see people wearing scarves in early September when it's 70 degrees out.

Devries' must have gotten their shelves restocked over the weekend because they had a good amount of stuff. I loaded up with as much as I could afford and could fit in the car. Other people were doing the same. By the time the first wave of shoppers had gotten through the small store, there wasn't much left. I felt kind of bad taking so much, but I guess if other people aren't concerned enough about their families to get out early do the same, well, then that's on them. All I can do is worry about us. I'm sure I'm just being overly protective. But the way I see it, why not? If nothing happens, then nothing happens. But if the wheels *do* fall off this bus, I'd rather be safe than sorry. Sure, the credit card bill for this month will be way higher than usual, but in my opinion, it's worth it, especially if we consume most of the stuff I bought. We'd have to get it now or get it in the next few weeks, so we'd pay for it eventually one way or the other. That's my logic at least.

Dylan – ever the little trooper – helped me carry all the stuff up the three flights of stairs to our condo and then assisted his mom finding space for it all in the kitchen cabinets. It took them almost half an hour, but now I feel pretty comfortable hunkering down for the next few days. I guess we'll just wait and see what happens next.

7:03 p.m.

Mmm…taco dinner.

Everyone's fat and happy now. Kate cooked up her special refried beans with Oaxaca cheese melted on top (I got mine with hot taco sauce). I have a feeling it's going to be a battle for the bathrooms tomorrow morning.

I have to write fast. Yep, I've gone and done it. I've turned the television off, and I have to move my butt before I lose my audience. I think that not having the television on is kind of a shock to the system for everyone. We've all gotten so accustomed to it over the years, it's almost like another member of the family. But with it off, there's no Su flu news coverage, no reality TV shows, no video games, no outside distractions. Sitting on the dining room table before me is a stack of board games – Sorry, Monopoly, Candyland, and Chutes and Ladders.

Dylan looks mortified, but I know he'll get into it once we start. Violet has already got the Monopoly money all mixed up and is playing "race-around-the-board-game" with the Monopoly horse challenging the sports car. Guess it's time to go play before Dylan deserts us and Violet starts losing – or eating – the game pieces.

11:05 p.m.

Everyone's asleep but me. I'm tired, but all this Su flu coverage has my mind racing and adrenaline pumping. Just sitting around most of the day hasn't helped. I haven't used up any energy. Plus, I think the tacos are doing battle with the refried beans and taco sauce in my belly.

All the news feeds are coming in from LA right now. Night has finally settled across La La Land, and the place is going wild. There's looting, there's rioting, and it looks like general chaos and pandemonium is ubiquitous. Cars are on fire. Buildings are on fire. People are shooting at about anything that moves (or doesn't move for that matter). Traffic on a lot of the streets and highways is moving at a snail's pace or stopped completely. Bodies are laying in the street (most of them look dead or close to it), and the overall scene is one of utter dissolution of law, order, and sanity. The police are trying to handle things, but it doesn't look like they're able to get a handle on the situation. According to reports, the governor has called up the National Guard, but supposedly they won't have the forces necessary to deal with the number of people going bananas there until sometime tomorrow.

I'm worried that the same thing will happen in Chicago. I know that our police and fire departments are good, but if what is going on in LA starts here, it could get out of hand quick.

Scary stuff...VERY scary stuff.

Wednesday, September 4th

8:32 a.m.

This morning was interesting. Over coffee, Kate and I discussed whether we should try leaving the city or if we should stay here and stick it out. We went round and round on the subject but never really came to a conclusion. I'm more of the mindset that we should get out of town after having watched the television coverage of LA last night. I put on the news this morning in hopes of getting Kate on the same page, but things there have calmed down now that the National Guard is on the scene, so it didn't look nearly as bad as it did last night. It didn't do much to support my case to leave the city. Kate felt that if things start getting too bad here, our governor will most likely call in the Guard too. Since we're a good 10 miles from downtown and in an upper-middle-class suburb, I just don't think she can envision things breaking down in our area like they did in LA.

I didn't want to push the subject too hard. And I have to admit, the thought of packing the kids up and hauling them out to the middle of nowhere isn't very appealing. Plus, what happens then? I mean, it'd be a fun camping trip for a day or two, but then what? What is the long term plan…spend a long weekend…a week? If things get that bad, I don't think they'll have shaken themselves out in a couple days or even a week, so what's the point of pulling up roots and running off to the wilderness? And then what if nothing happens? What if work and school resume and we are out in the middle of nowhere with no cell service? I'd be fired and a truancy officer would be waiting at our door when we got home wondering why Dylan wasn't in school.

While I don't think I'd mind a break from the city, both Kate and I tend to agree that with the kids in tow, leaving just isn't a very feasible – nor fun – sounding idea. So I guess we'll just continue to hunker down here for now and see what happens.

What do they call it, 'shelter in place'? I guess that'll be us. We'll be sheltering in place. I'd go get some movies from the library to watch, but after having checked their website, it appears that the library is closed until further notice. Great. Looks like we'll be watching the movies we already own. At least the kids have their tablets. They can watch stuff on those. Maybe I'll rent a couple movies through our cable provider too. We can have a family movie night – could be fun. I'll even make popcorn!

12:56 p.m.

I just can't stop watching this flu coverage stuff on TV. It's addictive and it's all over the place. Even during regular programming they're cutting in for updates. And now it's not just from cities around the US but worldwide.

It looks like hospitals, which are filled to capacity and WAY understaffed, are starting to shut their doors to people. This is causing even more concern among the general public. The hospitals don't have the personnel necessary to deal with the number of patients arriving, and those numbers appear to be increasing exponentially by the day.

The news is saying that the city morgues are full and they don't have places for the influx of corpses that are arriving due to the flu. There was even a shot of a parking lot outside Rush University Memorial Hospital where they had hauled in those big Dumpsters with the ends that can be opened up. They had plastic tarps over the tops and guys in hazmat suits were loading bodies into them. Sometimes they would just drive a fork lift with a pallet piled high with filled body bags right into the Dumpster.

They're showing cities like New York, Los Angles, Atlanta, and even Washington D.C. having the same problem. And I guess there still isn't a cure or any new vaccine for this thing. The CDC officials they keep interviewing don't seem to have a clue. They give their standard lines about people staying inside if and when possible, washing their hands, avoiding public areas, and wearing masks if they have to leave their homes, but it doesn't seem to be helping much by the looks of things.

The president is supposed to make a statement tonight. I guess we'll see what he has to say.

Meanwhile, back on the home front, Violet seems to enjoy having us all home with her. Earlier this morning, she and Kate played with her Fisher Price town set (the old one that I played with as a kid), and then she served us all brunch with her toy food set. It was sweet…something I don't get to enjoy when I'm at work. Dylan on the other hand is going a little stir crazy, but overall I think we're handling being cooped up together pretty well.

6:23 p.m.

Well that was a bummer. We pretty much got a whole lot of nothing from our president. During a dinner of burgers and fries, old fearless leader said about the same thing as all the news reports and CDC – stay at home, wear masks if you go out, do lots of hand washing, and they're working on developing a vaccine. He's got a conference call with state governors scheduled for tomorrow, blah, blah, blah. So much for that. Turns out, the president's daughter got the flu and passed away earlier in the day. Doesn't say much for surviving this thing if we, "the little people" of the world come down with it. If they can't save the president's own daughter, what's the hope for the rest of us?

After that downer, it's definitely time for a movie to get our minds off things.

9:08 p.m.

We ended up watching "The Incredibles" movie. We've seen it before…multiple times, but Violet is in that stage where she loves watching the same movies over and over; plus, we all love it. It's one of those feel-good family movies that has that ability to whisk you away and take your mind off things for a couple hours.

I made two bags of microwave popcorn with extra salt and butter, and we finished them both. It was a nice way to break away from the troubles of the world around us and enjoy some quality family time together.

After our movie, I asked everyone if they'd like to go on a special "night ranger" mission. I know that it's kind of dangerous going outside with the way things are, but it seemed quiet, and I figured that at this time on a Wednesday night, it wouldn't be too risky. We didn't do anything crazy. I mainly just wanted to give everyone the chance to get some fresh air and stretch their legs.

It wasn't a long walk, just a quick jaunt over to Devries'. I was curious to see what the situation was there. I also wanted to see what the rest of our little business district looked like.

In a word, it was "dead", even for a Wednesday night. We walked the few blocks to Devries'. When we got there, a sign on the door indicated that the store would be closed until further notice due to "supply issues".

Yeah, no kidding. I guess that's what you would call it when no one is coming to work because they're scared of catching the flu, there's no one to load the supplies on the trucks, there's no one to drive the trucks, and there's no one there to receive the supplies should they actually arrive.

By the time we headed out on our little adventure (a little after eight), it was already past Violet's bedtime, so we didn't make it a long trip; plus, I didn't want us running into people who might be flu carriers. After making a quick circuit of our tiny downtown, where the majority of the many shops and restaurants had followed Devries' lead and closed for the foreseeable future, we came home. It felt strange seeing our little burg looking like a ghost town, but it was kind of cool at the same time, like we owned the entire place or something. I think we counted six cars go by the whole time we were out. Usually, Main Street would be busy with traffic, even at eight o'clock on a Wednesday night.

The whole thing was weird…like something out of a "Twilight Zone" episode.

Thursday, September 5th

10:12 a.m.

This morning's news has brought more wild reports. It seems like things are starting to get crazy everywhere. We even had some problems with the cable and Internet this morning, and our cell phones are on the fritz. Kate was all in a tizzy since she wasn't able to check her online store. I tried to be supportive, but I eventually told her to just try to relax, there was nothing she could do about it. I know it's hard for her. Heck, I've been checking my work email almost nonstop lately. I've been very worried about our productivity numbers. It's amazing just how interconnected with and dependant upon our technology we are. I feel bad for Kate. She was afraid that she was going to start getting customer complaints if her store went too long without her being able to check in. Thankfully, everything was back up and working again by nine this morning, and she was able to log in and get things squared away. I could see her going totally berserk if she wasn't able to log in until tomorrow.

To try to keep tensions among the family to a minimum, I kept the television – and most importantly, the news – off, and put the radio on instead. I tuned it to the smooth jazz channel in an effort to create a mellow mood. It seemed to work, although I don't think the kids appreciated my efforts as much as Kate did.

3:15 p.m.

I had to sneak out of the bedroom to come write. Everyone is napping in our bed. We had a family backrub that seemed to put the rest of the group down for the count.

Never heard of a family backrub? Well, here's how it works…in our family at least.

24

Everyone starts on dear old Dad. Kate works on my neck and head (my favorite areas) while the kids chop, pound, kick, scratch, rub, and even walk on my back. Once they're finished with the old man, we form the family backrub chain. I massage Kate, Kate massages Dylan, and Dylan massages Violet. It actually works out pretty well, and by the time we're all done, the rest of the family is typically so relaxed that they're close to a massage coma and ready for a little shuteye. I on the other hand, well, I'm typically left wide awake and looking for something to do. Thankfully, I now have this journal that gives me an outlet even when everyone else is happily in the land of nod.

I don't think this flu thing would scare me so much if it weren't for the kids. If it was just me and Kate against the world like it used to be, this would just be another hurdle we'd have to clear. Back then, when we were just starting out, we had the ability to pull up roots quickly and relatively easily and do what we had to do to get by. But with the kids, it's not so cut-and-dry anymore. We're attached to this area. There's Dylan's school, his friends, his activities, and of course, my work. When I was in my early 20s, and still churning through jobs trying to find a role I could settle into, quitting one job and finding another wasn't a big deal. We didn't have many bills, we didn't have extra mouths to feed, and I didn't have to worry about finding a place with good schools and a safe neighborhood. Now it's all so much more complicated. And frankly, back then, if I died (which seemed impossible), so be it. I mean, it'd suck for Kate, but she could fend for herself. Now however, with kids who are dependant upon us, such thoughts about uprooting (or dying) are much more frightening, especially in an environment where it seems the world is severely out of whack.

This whole flu thing was kind of interesting at first. It's certainly not feeling that way now.

6:26 p.m.

Tonight on the news, they were telling people to stock up on bread, milk, bottled water, batteries…emergency supply type stuff. By the way things looked last night at Devries', it's a little too late for that now. I think that most stores are already out of a lot of those things, and the stores that aren't are closed either because they don't have the employees to staff them or they're afraid of people doing damage to their stores.

There were lots of scenes – both from around Chicago and in other major cities – of people looting the leftovers. This is especially prevalent in Chicago's south and near-west sides. There was even helicopter footage of several building fires that had been set and reports of widespread car-jackings and shootings all across the city. And of course there was the standard looped footage of people running out of broken store windows carrying flat-screen televisions, cell phones, laptops, small appliances, and other electronics – you know, all the necessities for surviving the apocalypse. People are so stupid. It's amazing we haven't met with some other major catastrophe much sooner. Then again, I guess we have if you look back through history at things like the Plague, Spanish Influenza, and Ebola. It's just been so long since such diseases have touched us here in the US that we've forgotten how dangerous they can be and have grown complacent.

Looks like a lot of people are trying to get the hell out of Dodge in the Chicagoland area…unsuccessfully I might add. There are scenes of streets that are jammed because a lot of the traffic lights are out, and the highways are a mess, packed with cars that have overheated or out of gas and have been abandoned. Makes me glad we didn't try to leave. I think it's better to just sit tight and try to ride this thing out. In all reality, I don't think we have much of a choice at this point.

The experts say that this flu strain is starting to spread like wildfire in just about every developed country. The only place I've heard where they're doing okay for the moment is down in Australia. They stopped air travel into the country yesterday, but on tonight's news they said that they've just had their first reported case. I guess stopping travelers was a measure that apparently came too late. If there's a first case, with the way this flu spreads, there's bound to be more.

I'm not really sure where all this is going. It seems like the numbers of sick and dying are growing exponentially each day. And with no cure or treatment, it's looking like things (no matter how they play out) are going to be pretty bad. They're saying that the death toll is already well into the thousands here in the US, and many hospitals are shutting down due to lack of staff. I don't blame them. A lot of their employees are either sick or are too afraid to go to work.

On television, the business channel was talking about the economic impact of the flu potentially running into the hundreds of billions of dollars in the US alone – worldwide it could reach into the trillions if things don't get better soon. The stock market is swooning and circuit breakers have halted trading today after a nearly 20 percent plunge in just a couple hours. I really don't care. I'm mostly just concerned about my job (from which there's still been no word on when we're re-opening) and my family. I mean sure, I care about my 401k, but it's not like I'm getting ready to retire anytime soon. If nothing else, this could be a great buying opportunity once things shake themselves out.

Still no word from the CDC on a treatment for the virus other than they're still working on it. Yeah, yeah, yeah. They'd better move their asses or there won't be anyone left to treat.

P.S. – No mail today. Don't know if we just didn't get anything or if this is a precursor of things to come – "Neither snow nor rain nor heat nor gloom of night..." but Su flu, well, maybe that will keep those couriers from the swift completion of their appointed rounds.

Friday, September 6th

7:42 a.m.

I heard gunshots last night. At least I THINK it was gunshots, although I'm not entirely positive. I guess I can't say with 100 percent certainty since I'm not used to hearing such things in my daily life. It was just after 1 a.m. At first I thought it was a car backfiring. But then I heard more, and then several in quick succession. By the time I got Kate to wake up, it was all over. When I asked them this morning, the kids said they didn't hear anything, but they sleep like logs anyway. Just as well. I don't want to worry Kate, and I definitely don't want to scare the kids.

I couldn't tell exactly where the shots/sounds were coming from. It seemed like they were to the east of us. There's kind of a sketchy part of town about six blocks from us, down where the freight trains run. Six blocks doesn't sound far, but it's far enough to be on the other side of the tracks. There are always people sitting in lawn chairs on their front porches or hanging out on the street corners with apparently nothing better to do. A lot of them look like young street punks and thugs. It wouldn't surprise me if a couple of them got together and decided to rob some of the houses up our way, especially if the occupants aren't around. I'm sure that the massive Victorian homes around our neighborhood look pretty enticing to people who are down and out. Heck, they look pretty enticing to ME! They're beautiful edifices, and a lot of them are filled with loads of lovely antiques and collectibles. If the doggone property taxes weren't so damn high here, I'd like to buy one for our own family. But that's living in Cook County. They'll tax the crap out of you and then ask for more. Wonder how much they'll have to raise taxes to make up for all the dead taxpayers and economic loss due to the flu? One day people are just going to give up and abandon this place. The city bureaucrats

28

can only ask so much of us as they piss our hard-earned money away. But I guess that's small potatoes in the scheme of things as they sit right now.

Anyway, the strange – or maybe "worrisome" is the better word – thing about it all is that I never heard any sirens responding to the gunfire. And living just three blocks from our local police and fire stations (which used to wake us almost nightly when they responded to a variety of calls), I'm sure I would have heard them. So maybe it WAS just a car backfiring. Sure didn't sound like it though.

5:15 p.m.

We got a sort of a wakeup call tonight (as if we needed it after all the news coverage that's been on). Posted on the various foyer entry doors of our condo building were notices from our local police department. They were requests for residents to stay indoors as well as notification that a village-wide curfew starting at 10 p.m. tonight will be in place until further notice.

Oh yeah, there was also a letter from the US Postal Service above our mailboxes. Mail delivery has been suspended until further notice. Guess I won't have to worry about that big credit card bill from all my recent shopping arriving anytime soon. Will the utility and credit card companies charge us late fees if we don't pay on time? It's not our fault since we're not getting mail. But I guess we could make our payments electronically. I don't really like doing that though since I have to give them all our banking information; plus, they charge us a "convenience" fee to do it. How convenient! It's not much, only a couple bucks, but it's more about the principal of the thing. They badger the crap out of us to "go paperless" so that they can save on postage and paying envelope stuffers, then WE get charged a convenience fee for such transactions. Just don't care for it, but now I'm kind of kicking myself for not doing it. Never saw something like the Su flu coming. I'll bet they don't charge people late fees. Customers would be in an uproar (those of them who are left after all this is said and done). I guess that right now, such minor inconveniences should be at the bottom of my list of concerns.

10:46 p.m.

I'm not sure what's going on outside. It must be something big. I heard sirens about 15 minutes ago, and I can see red and blue lights reflected out on Main Street. I like being up on the third floor of our condo building at times like this. Makes me feel safer. Plus, it gives me a good vantage point to see what's going on out on the streets. At least two cop cars are blocking the main intersection near the village hall, but I can't see what's causing all the commotion. Maybe it's just local law enforcement out ensuring that people are abiding by the curfew. Dylan's up with me trying to see too. He wants to go outside and look since it's only a block away. He doesn't get the whole curfew thing. I don't really feel like getting hauled in to jail tonight, so I guess we'll just have to wait until tomorrow and see if there's anything about it on the local news. I doubt there will be. There are so many other big stories taking up local news coverage time that I'm sure whatever is happening in our tiny suburb won't be of enough significance to break into the crazy coverage from downtown, the south side, and other big cities around the country. Still, my curiosity is getting the better of me.

11:13 p.m.

Jesus, what's happening?

I did something completely stupid. After Dylan gave up and finally went to bed. I snuck down the back stairs and across the alley to see if I could get a peek at what was going on outside.

I kept my distance and tried to stay in the shadows. I used a short cut-through between several of the buildings across the alley from us to get a glimpse of all the cop cars. There were at least six local patrol units plus a paddy-wagon from the Chicago Police Department. They were using fire trucks to form roadblocks at the intersections leading into our downtown. The entire main thoroughfare was blocked off from the train tracks all the way down to the library. The authorities appeared to be stopping all traffic from entering or even passing through the business district. Traffic coming in from other suburbs had to turn around and go back the way they came, and anyone on foot was being arrested and put in the paddy-wagon. The police officers were all wearing hazmat-type suits with protective hoods, and they were taking the temperatures of each person they stopped before putting them in the wagon. The people they were rounding up looked mostly like teenagers. They've probably got nothing else to do with school having been cancelled.

I don't feel good even just writing this for fear that it could get me into trouble down the road, but I actually saw them KILL a guy! Well, maybe he's not dead, but they sure as hell shot him. They had pulled him aside with a couple other dudes who they had already put in the paddy wagon ahead of him. They took this guy's temperature as they prepared to load him inside, just like they did his buddies. It looked like they were telling him something after they took his temperature and he started to panic. The conversation got heated, and he made a break for it, tearing away from the cops and starting to run down the street. Before he got more than ten yards, an officer shot him several times in the back. He fell right there on the street. I'm pretty sure he was dead. He wasn't moving at least.

That was enough for me. I turned around right and hustled home after that. I'm just glad we loaded up on food when we did. There's no way I'm chancing going back outside after seeing what I saw tonight. Tomorrow I'm going to take inventory of what food we have on hand as well as other supplies. I don't know how long this situation is going to last, and if we have to start rationing things, I want to get a jump on it. I'm amazed at how much food a family of four can go through. It makes you appreciate just how easy it is to get food at the store…or at least how easy it WAS…at least until now.

Saturday, September 7th

7:57 a.m.

Well, it's official. The governor of Illinois has declared a state of emergency and enacted a state-wide curfew starting each evening at 7 p.m. and continuing until 7 a.m. the next morning until further notice, not that any person in their right mind wants to be out of their home right now anyway. It's only those looking to loot, steal, or otherwise conduct the evil debauchery that the Su flu has apparently opened the door to that seem to be venturing out into the open. Honestly, I'm amazed it took the governor this long to call out the National Guard. I'm not sure how much good they're going to do. I think it's a little too late. Frankly, if I was in the National Guard, I'd certainly be having second thoughts about heading to the local armory or wherever they go to meet up. Heck, most of them probably can't even GET to wherever they're supposed to be the way the traffic lights are out and the roads are jammed with abandoned vehicles. Add to that, most public transportation isn't operating, and it's a real cluster.

Okay, enough writing for now. I'm off to do inventory. It's going to be a family affair. I want everyone to see what we have and know that this is it for the time being. They need to understand that we have no idea how long this thing is going to last, and what food we have needs to last us until things get back to normal.

8:11 a.m.

I decided to kill two birds with one stone and use my new journal to record this morning's inventory report. I'll start with what's in our cabinets and then move on to what's in the fridge. Here goes:

FOOD

- (3) Boxes Ramen noodles (12 individual servings per box)
- (4) Bags assorted chips/pretzels (some already open)
- (5) Boxes assorted cereal (two already open)
- (22) Cans assorted vegetables (corn, peas, green beans, carrots, refried beans, stewed tomatoes)
- (3) Cans black olives
- (3) Jars green olives
- (2) Jars jam
- (2) Cans corned beef hash
- (2) Cans corned beef
- (6) Assorted salad dressings/BBQ sauce
- (2) Boxes crackers
- (5) Jars pasta sauce/Alfredo sauce
- (5) Boxes pasta (1 lb. each)
- (2) Boxes shells and cheese
- (3) Boxes mac n' cheese
- (5) Assorted variety pasta sides
- (4) Cans baked beans/black beans
- (5) Cans mandarin oranges (Violet's favorite)
- (5) Cans peaches and fruit cocktail
- (3) 16 oz. jars peanut butter (one open, half full)
- 5-lb bag white rice
- (1) Box microwave popcorn bags (6 bags)
- (1) Box 10 granola bars
- (1) Container chocolate chip cookies
- (1) Box fruit chews
- (1) 32 oz. container oatmeal (almost full)
- (1) 18 oz. container grits
- 5-lb. bag potatoes
- (6) Bananas
- Assorted powdered milk, condensed milk, salt, pepper, spices, seasonings, bacon bits, biscuit mix, pancake mix, Italian seasoned bread crumbs, honey,

ketchup, mustard, whipped salad dressing, olive oil, vegetable oil.

LIQUIDS

- (4) 24-packs of 16.9 oz. bottled waters
- (2) Gallons distilled water
- (3) Bottles 64 oz. fruit juice
- (1) Box juice boxes (10 in total)
- (½) Case light beer
- (3) Bottles wine (2 red/1 white)
- (1) Pint bottle whiskey
- (½) Bottle vodka
- (½) Bottle gin
- (1) 12-pack soda

IN FRIDGE/FREEZER

- (2) Gallons milk
- (21) Eggs
- (1 ¾) Lbs Butter
- (2) Loafs white bread
- (1) 3 lb. pork roast
- (4) Lbs. ground beef
- (1) 3 lb. beef roast
- (2) Lbs. boneless chicken breasts
- (6) Pre-formed hamburgers
- (2) 16 oz. packages of frozen mixed vegetables
- (1) 12 oz. package shredded mozzarella cheese
- (10) Bun-length wieners
- (14) cheese singles
- 8 oz. package sliced ham
- 8 oz. package sliced turkey (about 6 oz. left)
- (1) opened 64 oz. orange juice
- (1) opened 64 oz. tropical fruit juice
- (10) Tortillas
- Assorted open condiments, pickles, butter, fresh fruits, preserves, olives, veggies, and a few leftovers.

Overall I'm fairly pleased with our supply situation, but I'm not going to get overconfident. It looks like a lot of stuff on paper, but when our non-refrigerated items are laid out on the kitchen floor, it doesn't seem like all that much, especially not knowing how long we're going to have to make it last. I think we'll start cooking the frozen meats and using up stuff in the fridge (along with some of the shorter shelf life items) just in case we lose power.

11:43 a.m.

Power's out!

Dylan's pissed. It cut right into the video game he was playing. He's moaning about how he didn't get to save his game before the console went off (like that's our biggest concern right now). Oh to be eight years old again! The world could be falling down around us (and apparently is), and a lost video game is his greatest concern.

I have used this opportunity to go down to our basement storage unit and dig out some of our camping supplies, which I admit, have sat unused since the birth of the kids.

But I'm glad I held onto the stuff. Some of it could come in handy. We've got things like our big camp cooler, the portable cook stove, three 16.4-ounce small-cylinder propane tanks to fuel the stove (hopefully they're still full), some candles and cigarette lighters (I pulled more such items from cabinets and drawers around the condo), and flashlights with extra batteries. From the collection of flashlights and batteries, I was able to get four working flashlights – one for each of us – just in case the power stays off into the night. We had to keep reminding Violet not to play with hers. She kept clicking it on and off, shining it in people's eyes, and generally being a four-year-old. To try to get her to save the batteries, we told her that shining the light in people's faces hurts their eyes. So what does she do? Takes it in her bedroom and flashes it in the eyes of her stuffed animals. Sweet little thing. I finally found a tiny flashlight that runs off a single AAA battery in our junk drawer and gave her that to fiddle with instead.

We also found a battery-powered camp lantern and a hand-crank radio/flashlight combo that was a present from our cousin one Christmas. We left things like the tent, sleeping bags, and cots downstairs in the storage unit.

Hopefully we don't need all this stuff, but it's nice to have it out and ready…just in case.

The city-provided water is still running, so I put Kate, Violet, and Dylan to work filling up some additional containers (pots, pans, Dylan's canteen, and some empty jugs and buckets). While they're doing that, I'm going to start cooking a beef roast (since our natural gas is still working too) as well as some of the frozen chicken breasts and mixed veggies. If the power doesn't come back on soon, I don't want to be left with a defrosted refrigerator full of ruined food.

5:08 p.m.

Power's back on now!

It wasn't too bad going without it. We had an early dinner. I gave Dylan the hand-crank radio to play with, and he was able to provide us with some evening dinner music while we enjoyed our roast. He'd have to stop eating every five minutes or so and give the thing a few cranks to keep it powered. It was kind of funny. The sound of the music would start to get softer and softer and then begin to fade out completely. Dylan would rush to get the radio powered back up, cranking frantically, before the signal was lost. It became a sort of game, and by the end of dinner, even Violet was participating in winding the crank.

As soon as the power came back on, I turned the refrigerator up full blast to get it extra cold, just in case it goes off again. I also began making extra ice and freezing some ice packs for the camp cooler in case we need to conduct a food transfer.

Kate and Violet are going to make popcorn tonight. I told them to go ahead and make all the bags. We can put the extra in a big holiday tin I cleaned out earlier today. Then we can snack on it whenever we like.

I put the television on as soon as we got the power back. The news said that there were numerous reports of power outages across the Chicagoland area and that the utility companies were having trouble gathering enough technicians to restore service to all locations. They also said that the number of flu cases was running well into the tens of thousands now just in the Chicago area alone. They explained that specific numbers on the sick or dead were hard to pinpoint. Many hospitals are no longer accepting patients and people aren't reporting cases of the flu since they can't make it to health centers or hospitals. Nationwide they said that reported cases were well into the hundreds of thousands and the total number of cases was more likely in the millions and growing fast. I guess the mortality rate for this thing is something like 90 percent and possibly even higher. I tend to wonder if even that number is correct, though, since I haven't seen interviews with ANYONE who has come down with this thing and managed to survive.

I've told Kate and the kids that we aren't going outside the condo for ANY reason! Unfortunately, there's hardly anything good to watch on television. It's all flu coverage on the news stations and major networks. All the sporting events from baseball and auto racing to golf and tennis have been cancelled. Most of the athletes don't want to participate, fearing exposure to the flu. Some of them already have it or have died from it. And no one wants to go to events where they'd have to sit shoulder-to-shoulder with other people in a stadium or grandstand. It's one thing to risk getting the regular flu, but no one wants to risk their life just to see a ballgame, car race or round of golf. And with as contagious as this thing seems to be, the chance of catching it just from being in close proximity to other people seems to be extremely high.

8:58 p.m.

The power just went out…again. It only stayed off for about ten minutes before coming back on, but it was just enough to give us the opportunity to test our flashlights and get a taste of what it's like to live in the dark. I tried to make it an interesting/fun learning experience for the kids, explaining to them that this is how the pioneers used to live ALL the time. I don't think they really got it. Dylan might have…a little. Having grown up in the country, where the power went off more often than in the

37

city, I'm more accustomed to dealing with such things than Kate and the kids.

Right about the time Kate and I got all the candles lit and the flashlights handed out, the power came back on. It was actually kind of cozy for a minute, but now I'm really starting to worry about what happens if it goes off and stays off.

Life without power for a few hours is one thing. Life without power for eight or ten hours or even an day isn't all that bad when you know the electric company will have services back up and running shortly. But when it goes off and you aren't sure if it will come back on in a day, two days, three days, a week, or EVER, it stops being a fun rarity and starts to become a real concern. More than that, I'm worried about the water and sewer services. I guess they have backup generators that keep these city services operating during temporary power outages. But how long can they last? What happens if those generators run out of fuel? We have enough food for weeks. But water is something we go through a lot of. We don't have any nearby ponds or streams. We have enough water to drink for a while, but how will we take showers? How will we brush our teeth? How will we flush the toilets? This could get messy – and stinky – pretty quick.

P.S. – As soon as it started getting dark tonight, I heard more gunfire. This time I'm sure that's what it was, and it sounded as though the shots were coming from several different areas around us – not too close, thankfully. Kate and the kids heard it too. I recommended we play a game of Sorry to take our minds off it. It helped. Dylan won, which made his night. Amazingly, the kids didn't seem too concerned about the gunfire, but I could tell Kate was. Frankly, I was too.

Sunday, September 8th

8:48 a.m.

For this morning's breakfast, we all ate big bowls of cereal with plenty of milk. I don't want us eating just to eat. And I don't want to use up too much food and over-consume. But at the same time, I want to try to start using up our perishables in the event we lose power for good. I'm finding that rationing our food and determining what to eat first and in what amounts is a difficult balancing act. I do have to admit, my stomach certainly welcomed the soothing milk to quell the stomach acid coursing through my belly. It was churning away at the lining of my gut while lying in bed listening to the amount of gunfire taking place outside last night. And unlike the last few times I heard it, the shots sounded closer to our condo.

The shooting started about an hour after it got dark and continued until around two or three in the morning. It increased in intensity before starting to dissipate in the pre-dawn hours. By this morning it was quiet again, although I've seen movement in the streets. Not much, but there have been several individuals running past our building, sometimes carrying armfuls or bagfuls of stuff. I'm assuming that these people are looters. And it doesn't appear as though the police are doing much to stop them from taking what isn't theirs. I'm not exactly sure where they're coming from or where they're going. I'd guess down by the tracks. And I don't know if its stores they're taking things from or houses. The positive thinker in me hopes they're not stealing at all. Maybe they're just residents fleeing on foot with their belongings. I don't think so, but I really have no idea.

What I DO know is that I'm having the entire family take showers this morning. I want everyone fresh and clean in case we lose water pressure. Things could get rather uncomfortable quick around here without water, so I want everyone as prepared as possible.

3:39 p.m.

The power went off just before eleven this morning and has been off and on ever since. It cut off once while Dylan was in the shower and he was hooting and hollering…it was actually kind of funny to hear him yelling about the lights having gone out. At least the water kept running and stayed warm for him. With it being a somewhat overcast day (which helps keep things cool without benefit of air conditioning), and with our bathroom only having one small frosted-glass window, he was forced to finish his shower in relative darkness.

Worse yet, the cable and internet were out for much of the day too. This meant that Kate was worried about work. Nobody is buying anything anyway. And it's not like she could ship the stuff even if they did, so I'm not sure what the big deal is. More than anything, I think it's the loss of control that's bothering her most. Besides her desire to stay home with Dylan when he was born, she left her previous work in accounting largely so that she could take more control over her life. Now that she's starting to lose that sense of power and control that came with being her own boss, I think it's kind of a rude awakening. I'm sure that taking the internet away has left a huge void in the lives of many people.

I haven't heard much from my own work. I've had a couple employees contact me wanting to know what the situation is or telling me they won't be in to work this week. I've tried to contact our regional VP, but I haven't heard anything back, so I sent out a mass email to our employees letting them know that as soon as I know something, I'd let them know. But at this point, the situation hasn't changed. We're still just waiting things out. I'm sure they're experiencing a certain level of anxiety, just like me. Will there be paychecks waiting for them when they go back? Will there even be jobs or a company?

I wonder how many of our staff have caught the flu…how many may not have survived? It's going to be weird when all this is said and done to see who made it and who didn't. Lots of funerals to attend. It's going to be extremely sad. I've worked with some of those people for nearly a decade. They're more like family than co-workers.

It's all so strange…like living in a movie. It just keeps getting worse and worse and there are no answers from anyone about what's being done to deal with it.

Maybe it's a good thing that Kate and I don't have close family in the area and that we don't communicate much with the family we do have. It seems like it would be much harder to deal with something like this if you had parents, siblings, or other close relatives to worry about. We can pretty much hole up in our condo and hopefully ride this thing out on our own.

We haven't heard anything directly from Dylan's school, but the last local news reports we saw said that ALL Chicago area schools will be closed for the foreseeable future. Local officials are urging parents to do their best to work with their kids as they would during summer break to help maintain certain basic learning skills. They advocate taking the chance to be at home to increase the time spent reading with children as well as to play more board games, do math exercises, and conduct similar educational activities.

So we took the opportunity to do just that. Dylan is reading "The Trumpet of the Swan" (I love that book – I still remember reading it in second grade), and he has a copy of "Charlotte's Web" to read after that. Kate reads stories and nursery rhymes to Violet from a Mother Goose book. And when I'm not writing in here, I'm getting back into the copy of "On the Road" by Jack Kerouac that I've been trying to finish for some time now. It's actually kind of nice. We all get our own candle to read by in the dull afternoon light. And while it's a little warm to make such a situation cozy, it's still a fun…well I guess I shouldn't say "fun", but a "nice" opportunity to spend some quiet, quality, family time together.

It's amazing just how deathly still it is when the power is off and everyone is reading or playing quietly. There are no fans, no blowers, no air conditioners running, no beeping microwaves, no running dishwashers, no washer/dryer timers going off, no chirping alarm clocks, not even the tiniest static hum of televisions or soft, almost indiscernible purr of computers. These noises have become such a part of our daily lives that we only really notice their absence once they're gone.

41

7:12 a.m.

When the cable finally came back on, the news wasn't good. It's not a pretty picture out there. The national news was comprised mainly of reports of death, dying, looting, and destruction from major cities across the US and around the world. The local news wasn't much different except that it consisted mostly of live helicopter footage of the looting taking place around the Chicagoland area. According to reports, a lot of people are already running out of food. Since the stores are all closed or empty, people are getting desperate and are now starting to break into homes to take what they can get. This is apparently acting to spread the flu to even MORE people. And those who aren't getting sick are getting shot at. It's particularly bad on the south and near-west sides of the city, but the violence seems to be spreading everywhere – FAST!

They're telling people to lock their doors and exercise extreme caution when it comes to "suspicious" persons in and around their neighborhoods. Huh! Looks like there's no lack of those! Suddenly all that politically-correct, be kind to your neighbor bullshit is out the window. They're also advising people that one course of action (since local law enforcement agencies are currently overwhelmed and understaffed) is to make it look like your home has already been looted by scattering clothing and other non-essential possessions around your front yard (if you have a front yard). The newscaster giving this particular report said that leaving an unattached garage door open could add to the façade that you've abandoned your home or it has already been looted. Personally, I'm glad we're in a condo building rather than a single-family home. We don't know our neighbors well, but out of our stack of six units (one of which is empty – a foreclosure), three of them are owned by single women, and the fourth is owned by a single mother with a teenage son. Plus, people entering our building have to come through the steel entry gate, across the courtyard, through our entry foyer door, then break through our locked front stairwell door (which I admit is glass-paneled, so it's not much of a deterrent, but it's a deterrent nonetheless), walk up two-and-a-half flights of stairs, and get through our inch-and-a-half-thick wood front door with three deadbolt locks. And coming up the back stairs would be even harder since they'd have to go through the steel door that faces the alley, up the stairs, and then through our own steel backdoor with another two deadbolt locks.

While I'm not naive enough to think that such deterrents would keep out someone who really WANTED to get at us, I'm also realistic enough to know that most robbers and looters are creatures of opportunity and will take the path of least resistance. I'm just thankful that our position offers substantial resistance.

I AM going to get the guns out, though, once the kids go to sleep.

6:59 p.m.

Watching the nightly news is getting intensely depressing. As if the constantly looping footage of the tragedy taking place around us, paired with the catastrophic events nationally and worldwide isn't bad enough, we now get the nightly mortality reports and celebrity death lists.

As of tonight, current estimates of those who have succumbed to the Su flu in the United States stand near four million, but even the mainstream media says this is likely a low estimate because so many people have died in their homes and have yet to be discovered. National estimates of those who are currently infected with the flu stands right around 10 to 15 million. Worldwide, they're saying the numbers of infected are already into the hundreds of millions. And again, those numbers are probably much lower than the true total of infected since they are mostly just educated guesses by the experts. Many of the world's bigger cities – especially those in lesser developed nations – are turning into gigantic cesspools of death and decay. The streets in these cities are literally filled with dead bodies. People are being infected and dying faster than the computerized models tracking exposure rates can keep up with. It only takes three to four days (sometimes less for the aged or very young) from the time the first flu symptoms are exhibited for the body to be completely overwhelmed. Apparently the virus moves from organ to organ, shutting them down and making it impossible for the host to mount any sort of defense. The ease of transmission and extreme speed with which the flu kills is making it almost impossible for anyone to find a treatment. Everyone the CDC has reportedly tried to test vaccines on dies before the vaccines have had time to fully take effect. Plus, I guess the CDC is now starting to run out of scientists and experts to work on vaccine development since their specialized personnel are dying from the flu too. Many of them were exposed during the early stages of the flu (all of a week or so ago) before they realized just how infectious – and extremely deadly – it was.

The only good news to come out of all this is that Washington D.C. is effectively shut down (I'm kidding…sort of). Congress and the Senate have taken leaves of absence (of course). According to reports, the President is supposedly still running the country (I hope they're using the word "running" loosely) from somewhere within the isolated confines of a secure bunker with a hyper-sensitive air filtration system. I guess this news is supposed to ease our worried minds. Sounds like the President will be presiding solely over himself pretty soon if he doesn't come up with something quick, although what that "something" is, I'm not exactly sure. He certainly isn't helping anyone around here as far as I can see. Still haven't seen hide nor hair of the National Guard. I'll bet they're all tied up – what few of them they could probably muster – down on the south side of the city. That portion of Chicago was a war zone BEFORE the flu, so I can only imagine what it's like now.

It seems like the new reality television programming is the non-stop news coverage of the flu. Instead of the hottest new celebrity gossip or the Hollywood hit-list of who's dating who being plastered all over the TV these days, it's which movie stars, television actors, entertainers, singers, musicians, or sports figures have caught the Su flu or died. The nightly news is a veritable who's-who of the dead and dying rich and famous. The news networks have a constantly running banner of not-so-long-ago, larger-than-life figures who have met their demise at the hand of the flu. It's weird to see eulogies or dates of passing for these figures, people who once played so prominently into our lives through the sports they played, the songs they sang, or the movies or shows they starred in. The heroes of the world are passing faster than we can keep up with…although at this point, I think most people have bigger fish to fry…like just trying to stay alive themselves.

10:16 p.m.

Just got done cleaning the guns. I hope to God I don't have to use them. Using the six-shot, hand-loaded .38 revolver doesn't bother me as much as the thought of using Dad's old duck-hunting gun. The thing is huge, heavy, and old. I don't think it's been fired in at least 20 years. I only remember shooting it once way back when Dad took me on one of his hunting trips. I was maybe only 11 or 12-years-old at the time. It just about knocked me on my ass (left a big bruise on my shoulder), and I refused to shoot it again after that. I've only got eight shells for it. I'm afraid that if I use the thing, it could blow up and do more damage to me than any intruders. I've got a box with 28 rounds for the .38. I'm more comfortable shooting that…still, it's been at least 10 years since I last took it to the range.

While I practiced loading both guns, I didn't keep them loaded because I know Kate would have a fit if I left loaded weapons around the kids. Personally, I don't think it's a good idea either, but I'm keeping them nearby and the ammo easily accessible in my top dresser drawer. I want to be able to get to the guns and load them quickly if necessary – I just hope it's not.

P.S. – I just heard some yelling in the alley behind our building. It was followed by several gunshots. It looks like someone is lying near one side of the alleyway nearest our condo building. It's hard to tell since it's dark, but the dark form doesn't appear to be moving. I feel bad. I want to go down and check on the person, but they could be infected or it could just be a trap to lure someone out there so that they can be robbed or worse. I tried calling the police, but all I got was a busy signal. I'm pretty sure the person is dead. I watched for at least five minutes and whoever it is didn't move once. I tried calling softly to the person from our kitchen window, but I didn't get a response. But I didn't want to be too loud and draw attention to our unit in the process. I'm not sure exactly what to do.

Uh oh, gotta go. Looks like the noise woke up Dylan.

10:56 p.m.

Just got Dylan back to bed. He had heard the gunshots and seen the body down in the alley from his bedroom window. Thankfully, he missed the part where the person was actually shot. Somebody came along about 20 minutes ago and looked at the body. Then they took what looked like a gun off it and left. It's still laying down there. I'm positive now that the person is dead. Great. Now we've got a dead body behind our condo building. In a sick sort of way, it could be a good thing. Maybe it will act as a sort of deterrent to others. Maybe they'll think we're a bunch of badasses holed up in here shooting people who try to enter the building. Wonder if they will remove it? Who is 'they'? Seems like local government and law enforcement have broken down. I don't want to leave a rotting body out there, but I don't want to mess with it either. It could be infected or something. Jesus, I never thought I'd be facing these sorts of problems. "What do we do with the dead body outside our back yard?" "Is that body infected with a deadly virus?" "Can the virus be transmitted from the dead or just from the living?" "How much food can we consume each day?" "Will the power be on tomorrow?" "Which gun should I use for the defense of my home and family?"

I haven't heard much activity from our neighbors lately. I wonder what THEY think about all this? Are they still here? Are any of them sick? What if the flu can be spread through the vents or between floors or walls? Shit…more fun questions.

Monday, September 9th

6:43 a.m.

The power went out this morning at 5:57. It came back on at 6:08, and then it went off again a couple minutes later. It's been off ever since.

With no electricity, I decided to make breakfast for the family. I guess "make" is a strong word. I got everyone bowls of cereal and then made a lightening-quick grab for the milk to keep as little cold air from escaping from the fridge as possible. We've now finished off one complete gallon and have just started our second. It's warm out this morning; humid too. It's stuffy inside the condo with the air conditioning off. The kids are already getting grumpy. Looks like a fun day ahead.

8:15 a.m.

The kids are complaining. They want to go outside. I feel bad for them. They've been pent up in here for too long. We all have. To keep the kids from picking at each other any more than they already have this morning, Kate sent Violet to take a bath. Vy loves baths. She puddles around in the tub, playing with a vast array of toys. She typically takes some of her toy cookware – pots, pans, plates, cups, and plastic foods – into the tub with her and spends time filling her pots with water, cooking meals, and feeding her rubber duckies, plastic penguins, and other tub toys. She can easily spend an hour or more in there, which is good when we're looking for ways to keep the kids entertained and kill some time during what have become some extremely long days.

Dylan is playing a game on his tablet (while the batteries last).

On a more serious note, I've heard coughing coming from an adjoining condo recently. It's extremely disconcerting. I heard it late last night, but I can't tell if it's coming from the unit beside or below us. I heard it a little bit more this morning at around seven, and then nothing. It's been quiet ever since.

I decided that I should make a run downstairs to take the garbage out (it's really starting to stink). Then I want to seal us in our condo. I don't know what's going on with our neighbors or just how contagious this virus is. I mean, obviously I already know it's highly contagious, but I'm not sure if it can spread from other units to ours through the air…like through the vents…and I don't want to take any chances. I'm sure I sound kind of nutty writing that, but when it comes to life and death, and especially the safety of my family, there's no room for error in my mind. Plus, with the electricity still off and not much else to do, sealing up the doors will give me a nice afternoon project…and Dylan can help me, which will keep him and his sister from fighting like caged animals.

9:47 a.m.

I loaded the .38 handgun. It was a strange feeling to load a weapon understanding that there was a distinct possibility I might actually have to use it. It was a feeling I've never experienced before. I'd say it's comprised mostly of fear (probably 80 percent) of being shot at. The other 20 percent is dread at the idea of having to use the weapon against another person. I know that if someone confronts me, I'll have to make a conscious decision, an almost instantaneous one: fire or hesitate. Firing means I might seriously injure or even kill someone. And taking a human life (no matter what the reason or situation) is not really something I want weighing on my conscience for the rest of my life. But hesitating could mean the loss of my own life – something I DEFINITELY don't want.

More than anything, I guess I'm just thankful to have the gun. I can't imagine being in this type of situation with only the doors to our condo building standing between us and what's going on outside.

With my gun in hand, I made a quick trip down the rear stairwell, out to the alley, and around the corner of the building to where the trash and recycle bins are. The body in the alley was still there. I didn't mess with it. I had Kate come downstairs with me and stay by the stairwell door so I didn't have to fumble with keys to get quickly and quietly back inside. While we were downstairs, we took a detour to our storage unit in the building's basement just off the exit door to the alley. There, I retrieved a roll of duct tape I had stashed. The brief excursion reminded me that I need to clean out our storage locker. It's getting too full of crap. It's filled to within three feet of the ceiling with boxes of books, toys, ornaments, bags of old clothes, and other junk that needs to be sorted through and either repacked or donated to charity. At least I've kept it neatly stacked and organized. But I'll leave that project for another day.

Anyway, on the top of my priority list is getting started on sealing us into our condo. I see no reason for us to have to go back outside in the next few days unless somehow things start getting back to normal…which from all current indications, doesn't appear to be happening.

Well, time for me and Dylan to get to work. I think he's actually looking forward to this project to give him something to do other than just sit around.

12:35 p.m.

Our condo sealing job didn't take as long as I thought. We took garbage bags and opened them up, duck taping them over and around the edges of our front and rear doors. Dylan and I did similar work in our utility closet, using some expanding foam insulator to fill smaller cracks around the duct work that runs up from the condos below and through our unit before exiting at the roof. It's something I've been meaning to do since we moved in several years ago simply for better insulation against heat, cold, and sound. I'd just never gotten around to it. I let Dylan be my "foam man", a task he enjoyed immensely, spraying the yellow sealant down into and around cracks and then watching as it expanded and hardened. Then we sealed the door to the utility closet (just in case we missed any cracks) with taped-up plastic

49

lining around its edges similar to how we'd done the condo's entry doors.

Finally, just to be on the extreme safe side, I found a can of disinfecting spray and gave it to Dylan. He went around the condo spraying everything down. Of course by this point, Violet was done with her bath and wanted to help spray. This started a whole new bout of arguing and fighting between the kids. It ended with Dylan chasing Violet around the condo trying to spray "her stinky butt" as he put it. But overall, we were able to kill a couple hours with the work and get ourselves sealed securely inside our hovel.

With that project done, I then took a couple minutes to remove the glass panel from the small bathroom window above the tub and replaced it with the summer screen to at least give us a little ventilation and fresh air. The problem is, now we can hear the distant sound of gunfire more easily – even during the day – which is disconcerting to all of us. Also, I noticed multiple spots on the horizon where black smoke was billowing into the sky. Looks like fires are burning out of control in some spots. I can see them the best out the back and side windows facing south and west. The opposite side of our condo building blocks my north-facing view, and the trees out in front by the street obscure anything toward the east. I would assume things probably look just as bad or worse closer to downtown.

I wish the power would come back on so that we could see the news reports on all this. I'm both curious and at the same time fearful to know.

2:26 p.m.

Well, I got my wish. The power came back on for all of about 10 minutes just after two o'clock. I flipped the television on, but we weren't getting a signal on the cable box. I tried our phones and the internet too… nothing. I even gave the radio a shot – nothing there either. Scary. All I can say is DAMN scary.

6:39 p.m.

I spent most of the afternoon cooking after the power went off again. I made burgers and cooked most of the remaining meat we had in the freezer. I just don't want the stuff going bad if the power stays off. We've continued to make extra ice since I began worrying about the possibility of a long-term power outage, and we loaded up the camp cooler we have. We put as much of the lunch meats, hot dogs, eggs, butter, and similar perishables as we could inside it. Then we iced it all down since the fridge is starting to get warm. But even the ice in the cooler is already starting to melt. I told Kate and the kids to go ahead and eat as much as they want of this sort of stuff since it won't last long the way things are going. Without power, and the way the summer temperatures are still lingering in the low to mid-80s during the day and only dropping into the upper-60s at night, once the ice in the cooler is completely melted, I'd give the meat a day or two at best before it starts to go bad. Thankfully, I bought some extra salt at the store the other day that I can use to salt the meat to help preserve it if necessary. I just hope it works. I really have no idea what I'm doing, but I saw it done on one of those Discovery Channel shows…Alaska something or other. I'm just glad I loaded up on some of this longer-lasting food when I had the chance. I hate to think what other people are doing for food right about now. Probably why there are so many places on fire. I'll bet people are starting to fight over the scraps.

P.S. – Oh, and by the way, we haven't heard anymore coughing coming from our neighbor's unit, although we did hear someone walking up the stairs below us this afternoon. It sounded like they opened and then closed a door either on the first or second floor. We didn't unseal our own door to find out who it was. I'm not taking any unnecessary chances just yet. I have to admit that I'm feeling rather anti-social and actually a tad bit guilty having not checked on the well-being of our neighbors. Still, it's not worth my family coming down with this hellish flu to find out how they're doing. I'll give it a few more days. If people are staying home like they're supposed to be, by then, we should know who has this thing and who doesn't.

9:13 p.m.

It looks weird outside tonight. I'm taking Dylan up to the rooftop with me to investigate. We had to wait for Violet to fall asleep since I know she'd want to tag along with her big brother if she knew we were going, and I definitely don't want her trying to climb up to the roof.

Dylan's so excited. It's almost as though he thinks this whole thing is some sort of game or Indiana Jones adventure. He went and put on his camouflage pants and T-shirt for the "mission" as he's now calling it. I'm not nearly as excited about it, but I'm glad he is. At least one of us is looking forward to this. I'm just curious to know what's going on out there.

We have to temporarily unseal ourselves from the condo sarcophagus we've created, which I'm not looking forward to; but if we do it carefully enough, we ought to be able to keep the majority of the tape and plastic around the doors intact. If we have to do a little repair work tomorrow, so be it. It's not as though our schedules are so hectic that we won't have the time.

9:47 p.m.

I had to come back for Kate. I wanted her to see what Dylan and I were seeing. I held a flashlight as Kate and Dylan climbed the steel-rung ladder leading up to the opening to our building's darkened rooftop. We aren't supposed to go up there, but what's the association going to do, fine us? From this vantage point, we could get a great view of what was creating the light we'd been noticing in the nighttime sky.

What we saw both amazed and frightened us. I guess those fires that we noticed on the horizon earlier in the day have spread all across the city. They were especially prevalent around the near-west and southern portions of the city from what we could tell from our position atop the roof. The flames from these fires were giving the nighttime sky over the city a strange, kind of eerily orange glow. You can actually SMELL smoke in the air, although it doesn't look like there are many fires burning in our immediate vicinity…which I take as a good sign. It looks like the nearest fires to us are possibly in Brookfield or maybe Countryside, but I can't be certain since it's hard enough to judge distance during the day, let alone when it's dark out.

It's weird to see the glow of the fires. Stranger yet is that the city seems deathly silent. Other than the distant smatter of occasional gunfire, there are no honking vehicles, no rumbling trains, no airplanes roaring overhead on their ever-present flight paths to and from O'Hare and Midway airports, no emergency response vehicle sirens…nothing. It's like the city is dead…and now it's being cremated.

Tuesday, September 10th

7:17 a.m.

The kids slept with us in our king-size bed last night. I think that seeing the fires kind of scared Dylan, and I can't say it did much good for me or Kate either. Kate wanted Violet in the bed with us after going up on the rooftop, so I went in and gathered our little sweetheart from her bed and put her in ours with us. It was nice (albeit a little cramped and certainly somewhat muggy) having us all sleeping in our stuffy bedroom. We haven't slept all together like that for years. Thankfully, there was a decent breeze, so I opened the windows to help cool things off inside. It was comforting waking up in the middle of the night and hearing the soft sound of the kids breathing. Every so often, one of them would twitch or jolt awake at the sound of gunfire, which seems to be growing ever closer to what has so far been our relatively safe and quiet little enclave.

Upon waking this morning, we found the power still out. Since the natural gas was still on, I cooked all the eggs we have left and used some of the deli-sliced ham and cheese to make ham, egg, and cheese sandwiches on white bread. I made each sandwich with two eggs. Dylan, Kate and I each had two. Violet ate almost an entire one on her own. I hard boiled the rest of the eggs just to have them cooked and ready to eat.

The stuff in the cooler is holding out. About half the ice has melted. This has turned the interior of the cooler into a soupy, slushy mix, but it's still cold, and that's what matters. We've been eating like royalty lately, stuffing ourselves full just to try to finish what will go bad in the next few days. The inside of the refrigerator hardly feels cold anymore. Instead of water or juice, we've all been drinking milk just to try to finish it before it spoils. We should finish it by lunch time.

9:49 a.m.

Boy, am I glad I got so much food cooked when I did. Our natural gas went off about 40 minutes after I was done hard boiling the eggs. Our water service went off too when I was about halfway done loading the dishwasher. I have a bad feeling that like the electricity, these city services won't come back on any time soon. I told the kids that we really have to start conserving our water supply now. I set aside a couple pots for teeth brushing (which we will only do once a day now and under parental supervision to keep water usage to a minimum). The dirty water from these activities will be kept in a bucket that we will use for filling the toilet tanks. I also explained that we will only be flushing the toilets once a day. The kids found that disgusting, but I told them we don't have a choice. Once we flush them, they won't refill on their own and we'll have to use our own fresh water to do so. I even took them in the bathroom and removed the lid from the toilet tank to show both of them how it works. I think Dylan got it; I'm not so sure about Violet. Either way, they know not to flush. I pulled out extra air freshener and told everyone to keep the bathroom doors closed to help contain any smells. I also taped socks on the toilet handles as reminders, since flushing is so ingrained in our daily routine. Then I went around and turned all the sink faucets in the kitchen and bathrooms to the "on" position so that we will hear the water running if it comes back on.

This is getting serious. I mean, it was serious before, but it's REALLY serious now. We haven't even been without water for an hour, but I'm already realizing just how dependant we are upon it. We can't wash our hands, do dishes, take showers, brush our teeth twice a day, or just get a drink whenever we want one. Thank God we filled up the extra containers with water ahead of time. Still, with four of us, I'm not sure how long what we have will last. Worse yet, our suburb doesn't have any creeks or streams running through it or lakes nearby. The only thing we can use for additional water would be rainstorms, and those can be hit and miss during September in Chicago.

I pulled hand sanitizer and some extra sanitizing wipes out for the family to use. We'll use them to try and keep things halfway clean and provide some feeling of freshness, but I don't know how far stuff like that will go. Having been pent up in this oven all day every day for almost a week, things are starting to get kind of stinky. And without water to bathe, and not being able to flush regularly, I think it's quickly going to get a hell of a lot worse.

Guess I'll worry about that later. For now, I'm going to get the camp stove set up and test it out. It's been years since we used it last, and I'm kicking myself for not having tried it out a couple days ago before we lost all our utility services.

9:54 a.m.

Whew! The camp stove still works – thank God! I have two small propane tanks for it that feel full and another that feels close to empty. I have no idea how long the fuel supply will last. I'm just thankful we have it at this point.

1:22 p.m.

I have to admit, not having electric service didn't bother me as much as not having cooking gas and fresh running water. Without those two things, it has been a real eye-opener. I can deal with reading books and playing board games as forms of entertainment instead of watching television. I can handle boiling hot dogs on the stove instead of throwing them in the microwave. I can get used to lighting a few candles and using flashlights at night instead of interior lighting…it's even kind of fun (to a point). I just never realized how pertinent natural gas and fresh, clean, running water are to our general day-to-day living. I have a feeling that most people don't even think about all the times throughout the day they just go to the sink to rinse a dish, fill a glass with water, or wash their hands. It's just an expectation to be able to flip on the faucet or flush the toilet, something we apparently have taken for granted for far too long.

By the looks of things, I guess the situation in the outside world isn't getting any better. Now that we've lost city services, I'm starting to wonder if we'll ever get them back. I mean, what the hell is going on here? Is this flu going to destroy the world? Is life as we've known it over now? I was planning for this thing to last a week…TWO at most. But now…well, I'm not sure what to think. Things aren't just going to fix themselves. If the people who run all these services and keep us safe – the government, emergency personnel, and all the rest – are dead or afraid to go to work because of the flu, how are we ever going to get things back to the way they were? And if we CAN finally get reorganized, how long is it going to take? Weeks? Months? Years? What are we going to do in the meantime for food and water? We're good for now, we can hold out a couple more weeks, maybe a month; but then what? Am I going to have to go out and hunt squirrels? It's not like we have a lot of wildlife and big game animals around this part of Chicago.

Okay, enough of these depressing thoughts for right now. My rant-writing isn't helping things. I think that with the way things are right now, we just need to focus on getting through each day. Every day seems to present us with a new challenge, and I guess that just trying to adapt to our ever-changing situation should currently be our top priority.

It's hot today. Worse yet, it's humid. We're sweating like crazy which means we're going to be drinking more water. I'm going to go see if I can't stuff some more food in the kids' bellies before it spoils, then see if they'd like to play a game or two of Candy Land, listen to a story, and take a family nap. The more we sleep, the less bored we are which means less fighting between the kids. Plus, when we're sleeping, we're not consuming our precious water supply.

8:42 p.m.

The kids are already in bed. I think they're feeling tired largely because they haven't gotten much activity lately. I wish I could take them outside and let them run around and play. I think Violet is doing better than Dylan. She's used to being home with Kate all day, and she putters about making us fake meals with her toy dishes and plastic food, dressing and undressing her dolls, painting pictures, or making things out of Play-Doh. Dylan, on the other hand, is used to getting out and having recess at school, getting to burn off some energy playing with his buddies, and generally being a silly eight-year-old. I'm sure it's hard for him being cooped up not just with his parents but with his four-year-old sister all day long. For me, it's so far been a kind of stressful stay-cation during which I've been able to enjoy more quality time with my family than I've had in a long time…maybe ever. The longer it goes on, though, the more stressful and troubling the situation becomes.

Kate's sitting here beside me on the couch, reading a book by candlelight. We're drinking warm beers. Thankfully, it doesn't get completely dark until around nine; still, I feel like we're living back in the pioneer days. Unlike our ancestors, we don't even have things like oil lamps or a fire burning in the hearth to help us see – it's either flashlights or candles…oh, and the electric lantern, which isn't all that great since it runs off a big battery that's pretty old and that we don't have a replacement for.

I made dinner on the camp cook stove tonight. It was actually kind of fun. I set the stove up on top of our regular stove, opened the kitchen window for ventilation, and had at it. I didn't try making anything too fancy. I mostly just warmed up some of our pre-cooked meat (pork and the last of the chicken breasts) and made some shells and cheese macaroni. All the milk is gone now and almost all the meat. There are a couple pre-cooked burgers left that I'll probably scramble for lunch tomorrow and put with a box of mac 'n cheese.

I spent a lot of time watching out the windows of our condo this afternoon and early this evening. There wasn't much to see, but that was kind of the point. I wanted to get a better perspective on just what was going on out there in our community, which from all outward indications, doesn't appear to be much. Occasionally, I'd see someone hustle past on the sidewalk or hurry through the back alley (the dead body is still laying out there by the way). Sometimes I could tell that the person I'd see was carrying a weapon – a rifle or shotgun or something. Other times, I wasn't sure if they were armed or not. What I DIDN'T see was any law enforcement personnel of any sort, and there were DEFINITELY no National Guard units present.

I also tried the radio again today. I got nothing but static.

11:02 p.m.

I went up on the roof by myself tonight. Things looked worse than yesterday. It appears that the fires have spread and are even closer to us now. I wonder if all the fires were set by looters or if some of them occurred due to people leaving things like stoves and ovens on (when the utilities were still up and running) before they succumbed to the flu?

Oh, and something REALLY stinks in our back stairwell. I'm hoping that it's just someone's garbage that hasn't been taken outside, but I don't know for sure. I really don't want to investigate.

On other fronts, I checked the situation with our cooler full of perishables on the way back inside from the roof.

It wasn't good.

There were still a few ice cubes that hadn't melted, but it was mostly just food packages floating in cold water. One more day and I think the warm weather will have completely taken over and whatever is left inside will be at the whim of time and temperature.

Wednesday, September 11th

7:54 a.m.

Well that was a fun night (sarcasm on full blast). I ended up moving all of us into the living room to sleep. I pulled the single mattresses off the kids' beds and put them down on the living room floor for Kate and Violet. I slept on the futon while Dylan took the sofa.

The reason for our change of sleeping spots was all the gunfire outside. It has moved closer...too close. I even heard what sounded like several stray rounds hit the building's brick exterior. That was enough for me. I realized at that point that it was only a matter of time before one came in through the window, and I don't want anyone in front of it when it happens. While they might be accustomed to such things on the south side of the city, we aren't where we live. And since the living room is positioned toward the interior of our U-shaped condo building, and the windows face the courtyard, it is far better protected from stray projectiles. The downside to this new sleeping arrangement is airflow or lack thereof. There's piss poor circulation for the stagnant air inside this part of our condo. This means that it is more stifling sleeping in the living room than in our bedroom. Even with the windows open, we just don't get the same sort of breeze. Most of our weather systems come in from the south or west, and our living-room windows face north. Any wind we do get from this direction is largely blocked by the units across from us. Worse yet, with the power off, we couldn't even put a fan on to help circulate the soup in which we attempted to sleep. Needless to say, no one slept well, and we're all kind of cranky this morning. Add to this, we're now largely confined to the living room since most of the other rooms have exterior facing walls and I don't want anyone passing in front of windows if at all possible. The kitchen only has one window on its west wall that faces out over the back alley. I moved the refrigerator in front of it so I can still cook there without risking getting hit by a stray bullet.

We make quick bathroom breaks, which works out since we're down to one flush a day and the smells are pretty unbearable. Kate even made airtight barriers out of plastic wrap to cover the seats in an effort to contain the stench. It's a pain to remove them, but it sure helps.

Kate is having the kids each make up a list of things they want from their rooms. They're working on the lists now. I'll make a quick trip to collect the stuff once they've finished.

The gunfire used to stop after daybreak, but now it seems to continue intermittently and from different positions around us throughout the day.

12:02 p.m.

We finished our perishable stuff from inside the cooler for breakfast and lunch. I saved the water from the melted ice. I didn't keep it for drinking since some of the meat juice and other food residue has leaked into it, but we can use it to flush the toilets, which everyone is definitely in favor of.

The gunfire seems to have subsided momentarily. Boy, I never thought I'd live in a time or place where gunfire arrived with regularity. The kids are playing quietly in the living room. The batteries are finally starting to die on their electronic devices. They're mad because I won't let them use fresh ones. I tried to explain that we need them for things like the flashlights and radios, but they don't understand. Violet doesn't get why flashlights are more important than her educational video games. Dylan understands, he just doesn't like it. Poor things are bored out of their minds. Dylan misses his friends. He said he'd even take going to school over being stuck inside for another day. That's how desperate he is. When Dylan – who is definitely no fan of school – wants to go sit in class all day, you know things are pretty bleak. Kate finally broke down and let them play on her work computer since she apparently isn't going to need it anytime soon. The battery won't last long, but every hour we can keep these kids happy and occupied is another hour we can retain our collective sanity.

2:51 p.m.

So much for the peace and quiet we were enjoying. At around two, there was suddenly a flurry of activity in the streets outside our condo building. Being on the third floor, and right near the heart of our little downtown, we can see all the way over to village hall that sits just off Main Street. From this vantage point, we watched as several groups of people, maybe ten to a dozen people in each group prowled the streets. They all looked like they were carrying heavy weapons – rifles, automatic weapons, shotguns, those sorts of things. A couple even looked like they had machetes. My initial reaction was that these people hadn't come to enforce law and order, and boy was I right. They started their destruction by breaking into the local hardware store. There, they got a hold of some axes and chainsaws which they then turned upon the plywood-covered entrances to several of our local eateries. Potter's Irish Pub was the first to go up in flames. I don't know if this was in reprisal for not finding any food inside or it's standard fare for these sorts of groups. The next building to go up was our local convenience mart, and shortly thereafter, I was dismayed to see smoke pouring from Devries' Grocery Store. It's currently engulfed in flames as are several of the Victorian mansions down the street from us.

As I sit here writing, I'm stunned by the senselessly destructive nature of human beings; but sadly, I'm not surprised. I think I'm going to take a quick trip downstairs and make sure our entry vestibule and stairwell doors are secured.

3:03 p.m.

I'm glad I checked our entryways. The vestibule door was still unlocked, so I locked it. I think that later today I'm going to see if I can find some wood in our storage area to put up over the glass panels in our downstairs stairwell door. I know it won't stop someone who is bound and determined to get inside, but it might be enough to deter them. I'm sure that...

3:42 p.m.

I had to break away for a few minutes. It seems that one of those groups I mentioned earlier found our building. About ten people came through the entry gate and into the courtyard. They didn't do much, just smashed a window to one of the ground-level units, screamed some profanities and racial slurs, and then ran out yelling and laughing. Looks like they're gone for the moment. I should probably do another check downstairs to make sure everything's okay. But first I'm going to do a quick rundown of how to use the shotgun with Kate and Dylan. That way, if something happens while I'm gone, or something happens to me, they'll know how to defend themselves.

4:29 p.m.

Okay, so I went down and double-checked everything. Both the vestibule and stairwell entry doors were still secure. I found a bike chain and lock and used it to secure our front entry gate. Then I took time to get a piece of plywood from the storage unit and screw it over the glass-paneled portion of our stairwell entry door. It's not the best done job in the world, but I didn't particularly want to hang out down there too long. Plus, there is a severe stench out in the stairwell. I'm almost sure someone has died. I'm not exactly sure what death smells like, but if I had to take a guess, I'd say what our stairway currently smells like is it.

So while I was down there working, old Ms. Murphy from 1B stuck her head out to see what all the racket was. She was wearing a white surgical mask, but other than the stink in the stairwell, she didn't seemed all that perturbed by what was going on outside.

She waved a hand in front of her masked nose and told me that even her mask didn't keep the stink out…whatever it was. The way she said it was so comical that I would have laughed aloud had it not been for the situation swirling around us. I didn't want to mention that one of our decomposing neighbors could very well be the cause of the stench.

Anyway, Ms. Murphy watched me work for a few minutes and then told me she was glad to see someone was taking action.

She said she had heard all the "raucous kids" out in the courtyard and was "…hoping one of us young folks would get up off our duff and take care of the building's security."

I asked her if she was doing okay. She told me she'd like to flush the toilet and wouldn't mind getting rid of the dirty kitty-litter from her cat…Felix is his name.

Once I was done with my work on the door, I headed back upstairs and got a mask of my own, a gallon of our dirty water, and a plastic trash bag. Then I went down and helped Ms. Murphy clean her cat box, filled her toilet tank for her, and took her dirty kitty litter away in a trash bag.

While I was there, I asked her how she was doing on food and water. She said that she was okay on food, since she doesn't eat much, but not so good on water. She only had a few bottles of fresh water left.

I don't really want to be giving out our supplies, but I felt bad for the old gal. Therefore, I took her down a gallon of fresh drinking water. She was very appreciative and thanked me profusely. I told her that if she needed anything else, not to be afraid to ask.

With the way things were outside, there was no way I was going to take the dirty kitty-litter out to the trash. So when I got back to our condo, I double-bagged the mess, made sure that it was tied shut, slid the refrigerator aside, made sure no one was around, and dropped the entire bag out our kitchen window. It landed by the corpse in the alley and exploded like a cat-poop-laden dust bomb. When it did so, several large rats scampered from around the dead body.

I have to admit, I'm pretty fed up with this whole situation. Any interest in trying to treat it like an extended camping trip or science experiment is over. None of us are finding this an enjoyable experience, and I think we can all agree that we are ready to have our old lives back. For as difficult, monotonous or frustrating as things sometimes felt before all this began with school, work, parenting or whatever, nothing compares to this. And I'm afraid that THIS is the new normal. What's most frightening about it all is that I'm not sure we'll ever get our old lives back. Watching neighboring businesses and homes burn is very disheartening, and not being able to do anything about it leaves me feeling extremely helpless.

What's next? God only knows.

5:16 p.m.

A late-afternoon/early-evening rain shower has helped douse the fires burning in our neighborhood. It also appears to have driven some of the looters…pillagers…arsonists, whatever you want to call them, indoors.

I'm using this reprieve to take a few containers up to the rooftop and attempt to collect some of the rainwater. Dylan and Violet are helping me. Currently, they're gathering containers from around the house.

5:47 p.m.

So much for my rainwater collection efforts. By the time we got enough containers set up on the roof, the rain had mostly stopped. I'd say we got about eight ounces of water in total. It's better than nothing, but not nearly as much as I'd hoped. I used a couple bricks I found on the rooftop and collected some paperweights and bookends from inside our condo to help hold our rainwater collection containers in place. I left them up there in hopes that the next rain shower will be more productive. We can use the rainwater for flushing toilets and even bathing.

For dinner, we're going to have sandwiches to try to finish up the last of the lunch meat. I'm going to warm up some canned veggies to go with it. Actually, I don't know if I'm even going to bother warming them. With the temperatures the way they are, they'll already be warm, and I don't want to waste the propane to heat them on the camp stove.

8:03 p.m.

Uh oh, now that the rain has passed and it's starting to get dark, it looks like those people from earlier…the looters or whatever they are, are back. I'm not sure how things are going to go down, but I guess I'll find out. They're coming into the courtyard now. I told the kids to stay quiet and in the hallway with Kate where there are no windows. I've got the shotgun and Kate has the .38. Gotta go make sure this doesn't get out of hand. I really don't want to have to shoot anyone. I've never killed anything much more than insects...although I did run over a squirrel once. But I'll shoot someone if I have to, especially if it comes to protecting my family.

8:58 p.m.

What I just watched from our living room window, was one of the worst experiences of my life. It was so surreal, almost like watching a movie...a horrible, gut-wrenching movie. It reminded me of the time back in college when I watched "Faces of Death", the movie (actually I think they made a series of them) of compiled real-life footage of people being killed – hit by trains, falling off buildings, committing suicide, and otherwise meeting grizzly endings – on film. I still remember the sick-to-my-stomach feeling I had after the movie ended. It's the same feeling I have now.

As I said in my last entry, those roving groups had come back and one was in our condo building's courtyard. It looked like it was the same people from earlier, but with the light fading outside, it was hard to tell for sure. They certainly acted the same. They looked heavily armed and were again shouting profanities. After cutting the bike chain off the front gate, they just kind of congregated in the courtyard, like they were unsure of what to do next. They smashed a couple more windows to the ground-floor units. I'm not sure if anyone is still living down there. I saw a couple of the looters duck inside the units through the broken windows, but from my vantage point, it didn't look like they came out with much. It was kind of hard to tell since, besides it being dark, I had the blinds down and was trying to peek through the cracks without really opening them. I didn't want to draw any attention to our unit or even our part of the building should any of the intruders be looking for signs of life.

So after a couple minutes of them screwing around in the courtyard, it started to quiet down. I thought the group was getting ready to leave. They slowly began moving back toward the entry gate, but I guess they were only taking a few minutes to come up with a plan. A few seconds later, a couple of them broke off and started trying doors. There are a total of five main entry doors to the front entrances of our building. Each door leads to a different stack of six condos. The north side of the building also has two ground floor units. They tried the first door to the north side, which was locked, and I'm guessing they tried the first door on the south side (our side) of the building (although I couldn't see for sure). From the brief amount of time it took for them to do so, I'm thinking that it was locked as well. I know for sure that OUR door is locked, since I'm the one who locked it, and I'm damn glad I did. Then they tried the door to the western stack of units in the center of our U-shaped building. It was also locked. But when they tried the second door on the north portion of the building, they got inside…and once one of them was in, they were ALL in. It looked like a swarm of hungry locust. They poured in through the vestibule door and then I heard the smashing of glass, which I took to be them breaking through the stairwell entry door.

By this point in the action, Kate and Dylan had come out of the hallway, curiosity getting the better of them. Thankfully, Violet was already sleeping. They were squeezing in around me by the window trying to get a view of their own. In hindsight, I should have shooed them away immediately in the event a stray bullet found its way up here, but I was so enthralled with what was going on across from us that I couldn't tear myself away. It was like a reality TV show gone terribly, terribly wrong.

Shortly after I heard the glass breaking, I could hear shouting and then what sounded like heavy pounding on wood, which I'm guessing was the group of hooligans breaking through condo unit entry doors. The front doors to our building's condos are all solid wood (almost two inches thick), but they can only handle so much. Most of them have had a single lock, and it's often not the wood of the door that fails when someone's trying to break it down, but the frame or the lock itself. Our entry door actually has three deadbolt locks for some reason. They must have been added years ago by an extremely timid former owner. I always thought them a tad overkill and somewhat ridiculous. Now I'm glad we have them.

Shortly after we heard the banging sounds, there was an eruption of what sounded like automatic gunfire. I'm not sure where the shooting started, but it continued for several seconds and then stopped. Then we heard more shouting and one of the windows was broken out on the second floor. About a minute later, we heard more banging, and then more shooting. This time, I could tell that it was on the third floor, directly across the courtyard from our unit. With the sun down, but with plenty of ambient light still available, I could see shapes moving inside the unit, people in front of the living room windows, and then suddenly flashes of light. There was the sound of gunfire, a spray of liquid (that I'm guessing was blood) against the living-room windows, and almost simultaneously, bullets that cracked through the window glass. Luckily, the shots must have been fired at an angle; otherwise they would probably have come into our unit. They impacted to the left of our unit's living room windows, and that was all she wrote. I immediately pulled Kate and Dylan away from the windows with me and we all took shelter in our central hallway.

Now the shooting has stopped. Violet is crying, and Kate and Dylan look terrified. I can't say I'm feeling much better, but I'm doing my best to appear calm just to help hold everybody together. I've pushed some larger furniture in front of our condo entry doors, and tomorrow I'm going to do more work to blockade entries to our condo and see if any of our other neighbors are still alive. It's time to get organized if they are.

10:13 p.m.

About ten minutes after the shooting stopped across from us, we heard more commotion down in the courtyard. It was the roving gang exiting the building and leaving through the front gate. They were carrying multiple boxes of what appeared to be canned goods and bottled water. I wish they hadn't found anything. Then they might leave us alone. Like feeding stray dogs, though, now I'm afraid they'll come back later looking for more.

They also left three macabre presents. They dragged what I'm guessing are the bodies of the occupants of the units they raided out into the courtyard. It's a horrible thing to do. I guess that's the point…some kind of mental warfare meant to intimidate and scare anyone else in the building. I won't let Violet and Dylan look outside. They want to see, but they don't need the mental imagery invading their dreams tonight. They've had more than enough for their innocently untainted minds to absorb today. Seeing dead bodies splayed unceremoniously in the courtyard won't do them any good. It certainly hasn't done ME any good. That's one of the reasons I've made some stiff cocktails for me and Kate. Now that the kids are asleep, it's time to down a couple of these drinks to sooth what have become some extremely frayed nerves.

Kate's kind of pissed. She says I've been writing too much in my journal. But this journal is my only outlet. I can't really talk to Kate about what's going on because the kids are always around; plus, I don't want to worry her any more than she already is. And I've got no one else to express my thoughts and concerns to. I can't even get away from everything that's going on by playing on the internet or watching some mindless television.

I need another drink.

10:46 p.m.

None of us ate much for dinner tonight. The events of the afternoon and evening left us all pretty wound up and not much in the mood for eating. It's weird; we can watch Hollywood films with all sorts of violence, shooting, death, and destruction while eating dinner or munching on popcorn, but seeing the real thing leaves you feeling like throwing up every time you think about food. You'd think that all the violence we've witnessed on the news and on television would have hardened us to seeing it in real life, but I can say from first-hand experience, that is definitely NOT the case.

I still hear shooting outside. Thankfully, it seems to have moved away from our immediate area for the moment.

I'm tired. Even though I really didn't have to do much to defend our condo, simply having our home threatened by armed intruders really sapped my energy. I need to get some sleep so that tomorrow I can attempt to meet with any remaining residents in our unit stack and continue to work on our defenses.

69

Thursday, September 12th

8:03 a.m.

The family ate dry cereal with the last of the bananas for breakfast this morning. It has cooled off a little bit and doesn't feel as humid as it has been for the past few days. It's still pretty warm out though. Blue skies don't help. The sun really warms things up throughout the day, and that means it probably won't rain.

We're still doing okay on our drinkable water supply, but water for washing up and flushing the toilet is dwindling. I siphoned some water out of our hot water heater tank this morning to give our two toilets another flush. There is generally a rush to the bathroom after a fresh flush. Everyone has realized pretty quickly just how unpleasant it is to be second or even third in line for the restroom after others have already used it. We've all started trying to hold it longer, especially once someone else has already gone in for a "code brown" as we've started calling them. I used the rest of the water I siphoned for washing dishes. They were really starting to pile up. We've used most of our paper plates and are now trying to eat sandwiches and the likes off paper towels whenever possible. It's amazing to realize just how many dishes you go through when you can't just throw them in the dishwasher.

Things seem to have calmed down outside for the moment, but it's still early. The intruders from yesterday haven't reappeared. Now that I'm done with breakfast, I'm going to don my surgical mask, take my .38, and make the rounds, working my way downstairs to see who is left in our stack of units. I don't really want to, but I feel somewhat obligated; plus, after yesterday, I unfortunately think we need to be ready for what happened to the stack across the courtyard to possibly happen to us. It's not an appealing thought, but this whole mess has been pretty damn unappealing.

I'm guessing that anyone who had the flu in our building has probably died from it by now, so those of us remaining in our stack should hopefully be safe. I just hope no one thinks that I'm one of those people from yesterday and shoots me.

11:03 a.m.

Well that was certainly more work than I expected. So here is a quick breakdown of what I found regarding the occupancy of the other units in our stack:

- 3A – Us
- 3B – Unoccupied. Someone has been working to remodel it over the past few months but apparently they have yet to move in.
- 2A – No response from Ms. Laurel, but there is a horrific smell issuing from inside…not good, definitely NOT good.
- 2B – No answer from Ms. Callahan. Not sure if she's gone or…well, gone.
- 1A – Ms. Williams and her teenage son Bradley are home and doing as well as can be expected.
- 1B – Ms. Murphy (and her cat Felix) is still managing just fine.

Ms. Williams is in her mid-50s, slightly overweight, but an extremely pleasant individual with an overwhelmingly positive demeanor (all things considered). Her son Bradley is a well-mannered, somewhat reserved boy, who wears glasses and has a bad bout of teenage acne going on.

I ended up convincing Ms. Williams and Bradley to move up to the empty unit across from us for safety's sake. That's why it took me a while to conduct my "meet and greet" and why I'm so tired. Dylan and I helped the Williams' carry their essentials up the two flights of stairs. I was surprised at how few supplies they had (especially when it came to drinkable water). I don't know how much longer they'll be able to make it without our supplementing their stock. We don't have much extra to give, but compared to them, we're a regular grocery store.

We couldn't convince old Ms. Murphy to move up higher in the building. She didn't want to leave her unit and she said she definitely didn't want to live with anyone else. I can't say I blame her. She's been living alone since her husband died nearly 20 years ago. I dropped off a few more bottled waters and a couple hot dogs I warmed on the cook stove since she has no way of cooking for herself. I also left her half our orange juice. Without refrigeration, I don't want it to spoil. She was very appreciative, and I told her I'd check on her later tonight. She asked about what had happened last night with all the shooting on the other side of the building. I wasn't sure exactly what to tell her. I didn't want to worry the old gal, since there's nothing she's going to be able to do about what's going on. Therefore, I just told her that there were some bad people out looting and that they had come to our building and broken into several of the units across from us. I explained that she needed to stay put and not open her door to anyone but me for the time being. I also recommended that she stay away from the windows since she apparently likes to watch birds in the courtyard trees with Felix (she has a rocking chair butted right up near her living room windows). The 1st floor units are just half a flight up and offer a nice view of the lower tree branches where the birds and squirrels often congregate. I explained that people were getting crazy shooting things around town (she might be old, but she's heard the gunfire) and that stray bullets were blocked by the building's brick exterior but could pass easily through windows. I also mentioned that if these people saw her in her unit, they might try to break in thinking she had supplies. She seemed satisfied with my explanation but said Felix would not be happy about not being able to watch the wildlife.

After we got done relocating the Ms. Williams and her son, we moved an extra sofa from their unit out into the stairwell, leaving it in the stairway between the entry door and where the stairs begin. It creates a pretty good obstacle. While it might not stop intruders from getting inside and up the stairs, like the plywood I put over the entry door, it will certainly slow their advance and make life more difficult for them. I've heard that with looters, it's often just a simple deterrent that is enough to push them on to easier pickings because they're looking for quick and easy access to their targets.

I can only pray that what I've heard is correct.

12:23 p.m.

So far, things seem a little calmer outside today. But now we have a new problem to contend with. The stench issuing from Ms. Laurel's condo is absolutely horrific. Something has to be done, and I'm afraid I'm going to be the one who has to do it. I really don't want to go down there, but if I don't, we're not going to be able to stay here. The smell is overpowering, and no matter how much air freshener we spray, it never goes away. It's seeping into everything, everywhere. The kids are dying, constantly gagging and complaining. Even our food is starting to absorb the smell, and when we try to eat (a desire we're having less frequently since the smell is destroying our appetites), the food tastes absolutely disgusting.

1:17 p.m.

What I just got back from was one of the most disgusting things I've ever had to go through.

I handed out medical face masks and handkerchiefs to help with blocking the stench and then took Kate and Bradley (Ms. William's 16-year-old son) downstairs where we broke into Ms. Laurel's second-floor unit directly below ours. At the time, I didn't think that the smell could get worse…I was wrong. Inside the unit, it was a hot, steamy, stink-bath.

After a few seconds of retching and dry-heaving, I left Kate and Bradley in the hallway and went inside. It didn't take long to find Ms. Laurel…what was left of her at least. I followed the sound of swarming flies into the living room. She was laid out on the sofa and very badly decomposed. I almost lost it when I found her. The maggots were doing their best to make quick work of her. The sight and smell were overwhelming, and I had no desire for anyone else to have to suffer through what I was experiencing. Therefore, I found a blanket to cover her with, then I went back and got Kate and Bradley to assist me.

We had to get the body outside to rid ourselves of the stench of death that was overwhelming our building. The problem we found ourselves facing was that we had a body in the midst of decomposition, in an upstairs condo unit, in a building that

73

currently had the doors locked, in a neighborhood that was literally under attack by roving gangs of some apparently very dangerous people.

The first obstacle we faced was getting poor Ms. Laurel's body off the couch. She was a gelatinous blob of body fluids and decomposing flesh. The second problem was that we were on the second floor of the condo building. We had no desire to carry the disgusting mess Ms. Laurel presented downstairs, risking covering ourselves in bodily sludge along the way, in turn, possibly exposing ourselves to unknown and potentially deadly pathogens along the way. Thankfully, Ms. Laurel was lying on a blanket on the sofa, but we didn't want to try to move her far since we were afraid she'd start coming apart on us along the way. We therefore maneuvered a big comforter onto the floor beside the sofa. Then we pulled the sofa cushions (with the remains of Ms. Laurel still on them) down onto the comforter. Once we had her positioned, we bound the comforter around the remnants with some heavy string we found in the kitchen. Then, we quickly (since the smell was threatening to overpower us, even with our face masks on) moved the entire mess into the kitchen. From there, we opened the kitchen window and hefted Ms. Laurel's wrapped and tied body up and out the window.

It was a sad and certainly unceremonious funeral, but it was really the best we could do considering the circumstances. As Ms. Laurel landed, she splashed a stray dog that was sniffing around the other body in the back alley. Now we have two bodies in the alley and three in the front courtyard. What is our world coming to and how bad is the smell going to get? We felt terrible about the whole situation, but we consoled ourselves with the fact that Ms. Laurel is hopefully in a better place now. And what the hell else are we supposed to do? It's not like they teach you how to handle this kind of stuff in school or at work.

Looks like I'm going to have to go back outside later tonight and try to move the corpses away from our building to try to keep the smell to a minimum. Yet another activity I'm not looking forward to.

We left all the windows in Ms. Laurel's unit open to try to air the place out, and we threw anything else that had been saturated by body fluid out the kitchen window. If nothing else, hopefully the things we tossed out will act as a deterrent to others trying to get into our building. The smell alone would be enough to keep me away if I didn't have to live here.

Just as we finished with our grizzly work, we heard gunshots nearby. I took Bradley back upstairs to his mom, where I told them to lock themselves in their new condo. Before I left, I checked their rear entry stairs. All the B side units in our stack exit to an open-air staircase that is protected by a caged gate at the bottom. The gate is locked, but it's not quite as secure as the A-units' enclosed rear stairwell, the bottom of which is fitted with a steel door built into the building's brick exterior. However, I double-checked that the street-level entry gate was closed and locked, and I chained it shut with a bike lock I found down there. With this done, I waited in the stairway landing separating our two units until I heard the Williams' lock themselves in before heading back to my own unit. They don't have a weapon, and neither of them know how to use a gun, so I guess it's up to me to act as communal security guard.

5:07 p.m.

I made the last of the hot dogs tonight and opened several cans of baked beans. The kids were happy with the hot dogs – not so much with the beans. Violet absolutely refused to touch them. Finally, not wanting to waste food, I mashed them up for her and drizzled maple syrup over top of them. Then she was at least willing to have a few bites before Dylan finished them for her.

I took several of the dogs and one can of beans over to Ms. Williams and Bradley, then I took some down to Ms. Murphy too. All were very appreciative. I didn't want to tell them that I did it mostly because I was afraid the hot dogs were going to go bad if we didn't use them soon. I served the hot dogs rolled up in tortillas (several of which were already molded and had to be tossed) instead of buns since we were out of buns and I realized that the remaining tortillas weren't likely to last much longer. I noticed that many of the potatoes in our 5-lb bag were starting to sprout (several on the bottom of the bag had gone soft), but there isn't much I can do about it. I don't want to waste the propane boiling a bunch of potatoes, and we're not desperate enough to eat them raw, so I guess they're going to go the route of poor Ms.

75

Laurel – out the window. I think our remaining butter is soon headed in that direction as well, although when I was a kid, I remember my grandparents leaving butter out on the kitchen table for extended periods of time, so I'm not really sure how long it will last. These summer temps and the humidity of the past few days aren't doing much to help our food preservation efforts.

My own dinner on the other hand consisted of a can of fruit cocktail. It was about all I could stomach considering that I was still suffering from olfactory post-traumatic stress due to the whole Ms. Laurel debacle. Every time I think of eating something solid (especially something like hot dogs), I start having visions of her lying on her couch, her face full of wriggling, writhing maggots, and that horrible smell would come wafting back to me. The soft canned fruit was the only thing I could force myself to ingest.

9:14 p.m.

It was reasonably quiet throughout the majority of the early evening hours. Gunfire, while ever-present now, was held largely to a minimum and was distant enough not to be too worrisome. Huh, that's not something I ever thought I'd write, the gunfire was "distant enough not to be too worrisome." Boy, that's great. What a world we live in now.

Anyway, at around seven this evening, we temporarily moved the mattresses out of the living room and invited our neighbors over. Ms. Williams (who's first name we now know is Brenda) and Bradley arrived first. Ms. Murphy (who later in the evening I found out was approaching her 80th birthday in the next few weeks) even made the trip up the two flights of stairs to visit our condo.

We lit candles, mostly provided by Ms. Murphy (she's an old-school kind of gal who likes burning candles even when the apocalypse ISN'T upon us), broke out the playing cards and board games, and made a night of it. Kate whipped up some hors d'oeurves – nothing fancy, just some peanut butter on crackers, green and black olives, chips, pretzels, and sweet pickles, but everyone seemed to enjoy them.

Our cozy atmosphere made for a pleasant evening, and had it not been for the circumstances surrounding the situation, we might actually have really enjoyed ourselves. But I could tell that other than Violet, Dylan, and Ms. Murphy (who maybe I should rename "Old Ironsides" due to her unflappable personality), the rest of us were on edge. Kate, Brenda, and I would all look nervously toward the nearest window whenever gunfire erupted, but old Ms. Murphy stayed focused purely on the game, almost as though there was money was at stake. She's definitely one tough old bird.

While we played cards, Bradley played board games with Violet and Dylan. I think they liked having another kid – albeit a significantly older one – to spend time with. And Bradley was great with them.

It made me wish we'd made these contacts with our neighbors before the flu. Everyone stayed to themselves before. It's a shame that it took something as horrendous as this to bring us all together.

10:38 p.m.

After the kids fell asleep, Kate and I had some time to talk. It wasn't a fun conversation, but it was one we needed to have, although I'm not sure it really got us anywhere. We discussed our future, the kids' futures, the world's future, and what our plan should be moving forward. I can't say we came up with much. Having been cut off from any source of outside news for the last few days, we really have no idea what's going on in our little suburb of Chicago let alone the rest of the city or across the nation. From all outward indications (burning fires, gunfire, and roving gangs of killers), it's not looking too good here. Therefore, I'd have to imagine it's not much better in the rest of Chicago, and I'm willing to assume it's probably about the same in other major cities. What it's like in smaller towns and rural areas, well, one can only guess – might be better. I can't imagine it being worse.

Kate and I both agreed that we really don't have any other option at the moment other than to continue sheltering in place. If we can wait this thing out, maybe people will get some sort of governing structure or at least a little law and order in place…although I have my doubts the way things have been looking outside lately. After the attack on our condo building the other day, it seems we're still far from things shaking themselves out.

I mentioned to Kate that if things stay calm tomorrow, maybe I should go out and see if I can meet up with someone from around town who might know more about what's going on. She wasn't thrilled with the idea, but I think we're both dying to know more about what's happening here as well as what the overall situation is in and around Chicago. Being cut off and in the dark regarding how the rest of the world is doing leaves us feeling so helpless. Before all this, with the internet, our phones, and 24-hour news coverage, we had so much information at our fingertips, it was ridiculous. Now we have absolutely nothing. And with the way things are going with our supplies, I'd give us another couple weeks with the food we have left (especially if we have to continue helping out our neighbors), and probably less than that with drinkable water. It looks like pretty soon we're going to have to drain the rest of our water heater tank for extra drinking water. I can also boil rainwater…if it ever rains again.

Friday, September 13th

8:07 a.m.

Eight o'clock in the morning. All quiet on the western front.

Breakfast was grits with butter (lots of butter since we're trying to use it up) and salt. I made us a big pot on the camp stove. It's a filling meal but is better suited to winter as it really warms a body up.

I took a few minutes to check on Ms. Murphy after we finished eating. She seems to be doing just fine. She was having bread and butter with a glass of room temperature tea. At least she doesn't eat much. Ms. Murphy (whose first name I learned last night is Elaine, but I prefer "Ms. Murphy") was breaking off little bits of bread and feeding them to her cat, Felix, a mottled tabby. I think Felix is about as old as Ms. Murphy – in cat years that is.

I told the old dear (Ms. Murphy, not Felix) that I'd come back later in the day and clean the cat box for her. I know she could do it herself, but it gives me an excuse to check on her. She just smiled and said, "You're such a sweet lad." I think she likes the company more than anything.

Today is bath day for our family. I guess the word "bath" is somewhat extreme.

We've come up with a system. It's actually quite a little production. For once, I'm glad it's warm out so that I don't have to waste propane heating water. Cooler water actually feels nice in the late-summer heat.

I liken our bathing process to doing dishes before dishwashers became the norm…or after the flu took such amenities from us. So here's how it goes.

We filled a gallon bucket with soapy water and a washcloth to clean with. Then we filled another gallon bucket with plain water and a washcloth for rinsing. We started with Kate washing

Violet. After she was done, Dylan went, then Kate, and I finished. We got in the tub, one after the other, washing ourselves from the first bucket and rinsing from the second. I even allowed myself a small cup of water to shave with, something I hadn't done in days. I would have left my scruff in an effort to conserve water, but it is extremely itchy and was driving me a little bit crazy, especially in this summer heat.

The overall results of our bathing efforts weren't great, but all things considered, I guess they're the best we could hope for. Most of all, I'm just thankfully to be rid of my days-old stubble. Ugh! It was terrible.

10:41 a.m.

Dylan and I spent the morning reorganizing and re-inventorying our food stocks while Kate and Violet played together in the living room. We took time to sort through the food, not just getting a tally of what we have left, but also inspecting it for freshness – putting several items into air-tight containers – and looking for signs of mold.

Most of the containers we filled before we lost city water service are now empty. We drained the last few into sealable bottles and then refilled them from whatever was left in the hot water heater tank. We did this to give any sediment remaining in the tank's water time to settle.

It's kind of strange, I wouldn't think we'd be so busy with nothing to do relating to school, work, or activities for the kids, but the simple act of survival without modern amenities and conveniences is a lot more time consuming and much harder work than I ever expected. And such efforts seem to get tougher with each passing day. Things like personal hygiene, food preparation, and just keeping dishes and our living space clean and sanitary take up so much of our time now. It really makes you appreciate what we have...HAD I guess I should say. What's the line? "You don't know what you've got 'til it's gone." That's pretty applicable to our living situation right about now.

1:19 p.m.

So far, so good. Today has been fairly calm. It's cooler outside with a nice breeze, and it has remained relatively quiet. I'd say it almost seems like a normal day other than the dead bodies surrounding the building and the occasional smatter of distant gunfire.

Today's lunch was peanut butter and jelly sandwiches (we used up the last of the bread and finished the first of our jars of peanut butter as well as a jar of jelly in the process), a can of mandarin oranges, some chocolate chip cookies, the last of the granola bars, some potato chips, and fruit juice. It reminded me of the picnic we had in Riverside during Labor Day weekend – it seems like so long ago.

We lent the portable cook stove to Brenda and Bradley and gave them a couple packs of Ramen noodles and some of our potato chips since they're almost out of food. I asked them to utilize water from the hot water tank in their unit to cook with. As usual, they were appreciative, but I can tell they're having trouble accepting our charity. And while I don't want to say anything, I'm starting to wonder how long we're going to have to support them. It's hard enough taking care of my own family, let alone throwing two more, what I consider adults (since they eat as such) into the mix. I don't want to be rude or appear heartless, but when it comes to a situation that is becoming more life-or-death by the day, and where food and water is scarce, they could cut our remaining food supply by days or even weeks. I feel for them, but if it means taking food from my own kids' mouths, we might have to reconsider the situation. For now, though, we have enough to spare, and hopefully things will somehow get resolved before we have to make any tough decisions.

I made a quick trip downstairs to visit Ms. Murphy after lunch. I took her a sandwich and bottled water (yet another drain on our resources). While I was in her unit, I took time to fill her up several buckets of water from her own hot water heater tank. I'm thankful to have thought of this valuable water resource, since without it, I'm not sure what we'd do for extra water. I brought a jar of green olives with me for Felix since Ms. Murphy mentioned the other night that he has liked them as special treats since he was a kitten. I changed the litter box for her too. I have to admit, that

81

chore is already getting old. It's bad enough having to deal with our own family's waste, let alone a cat's.

Oh the joys of being stuck indoors all day.

6:33 p.m.

Tonight I invited our neighbors for dinner. I boiled a pound of noodles (I now have a pot of what I call "my boiling water" that I use solely for the purpose of boiling pasta). I mixed the noodles with a jar of spaghetti sauce and used it to feed our entire extended family of condo residents. It wasn't the most exciting meal in the world, but I livened up the sauce with a little extra Italian seasoning and threw in a bit of garlic salt. I also used up most of the remaining butter since Violet and Dylan like their pasta with just butter and salt.

We tried to keep the conversation light and away from subjects like the flu, lost friends and family, and the future. All in all, it was a satisfying meal and it seemed to fill everyone up. However, tonight, we didn't play games after dinner. Something else was vying for our attention. It seems that a large fire has been set out on Main Street. We can't see exactly where it is or what's burning, but it looks very close to the intersection of Main Street and 7th Ave. right at the heart of our little downtown. I'm not sure if it's a car, multiple cars or something else. I'm curious as hell – as is everyone else – to know what it is, but I'm afraid it might be some sort of trap. It might just be a way to lure people outside. On the other hand, it could be an attempt to get people from the community to rally together. I'm just not sure. What I AM sure of is that I don't want to hide inside when there might be efforts underway to start getting things back to some sense of normalcy or at least secure our neighborhood from further danger.

7:05 p.m.

Okay, I can't take it any longer. I've been watching the smoke rise out on the street and it's driving me nuts wanting to know what it is. And now I can see people coming and going from whatever is burning. I think it's time to take a chance. Now that

82

the sun is starting to go down, I might risk venturing outside. I think I'll wait just a little bit longer, maybe until around seven-thirty. With dusk approaching, I can use the poor lighting to my advantage. I'll keep to the shadows, sneak a peek at what's going on, and then make a decision as to what I want to do from there.

Bradley wants to come with me, but his mother is against it. I'm against it too for that matter. It's not that I don't want some backup along the way, but with him not knowing how to handle a weapon, I'm not confident he'd be much help. He might end up slowing me down, so I think it's best to go alone.

8:59 p.m.

Well that was interesting. I have a lot to write about this evening.

So I guess I should start with the fact that I DID actually venture outside tonight. I waited until just after 7:30. Once the sun had gone down far enough that it provided some good shadows for cover, I took my .38 and snuck out the rear exit of our condo building. I had to make my way past the still wrapped and bound Ms. Laurel and the remains of the dead person next to her that have largely been picked apart by wandering wildlife.

I cut between several buildings across the alley from ours and made my way out to Main Street. There, I could see several people wearing face masks and gloves grouped around a large bonfire set in the middle of the street. Several more people were bringing things in wheelbarrows to add to the fire.

After watching for a minute, I realized that those "things" were human bodies. They were actually BURNING bodies. I couldn't believe it at first, but after thinking about it, it made sense. I mean, what the hell else are we supposed to do with all our dead? There have got to be so many around now that it would be impossible for survivors to bury them all. And we need to get rid of the remains to help keep conditions somewhat sanitary. Before we lost power, I remember news reports about the city morgues and hospitals being filled to capacity with flu victims. I guess I shouldn't be surprised that this is what it has come to.

After watching what was going on for a few minutes, the situation didn't appear dangerous. And I thought I recognized one of the people working when he temporarily removed his mask to wipe away some sweat, so I decided to take a chance.

It turned out that the person I thought I recognized was Scott Anderson, the father of one of Dylan's friends. We'd met and had several conversations at practices and games when Dylan and Scott's son, Finn were on the same basketball team last year.

After making a quick introduction, Scott explained that he had lost his mother and father to the flu but that his wife Selma, and their kids, Finn and Liam had thankfully remained untouched. He went on to tell me that a lot of his neighbors (they live several blocks away on 8th Avenue) hadn't been so lucky. In fact, many of them had succumbed to the flu. He and a few of his remaining neighbors – Issac Franz and Jim Abrel – had been working a several block radius around their homes seeing who was still alive. Unfortunately, I guess they haven't been having much success, finding mostly decaying corpses. Those who ARE still alive are burdened with the rotting remains of passed family members, thus the bonfire this evening. Cremation was the most efficient method they could come up with on the spur of the moment. Scott and his two neighbors had undertaken the depressing task of trying to clear the immediate vicinity around their own houses of decomposing bodies.

I told him about the two in our alley and the three in our front courtyard and he lent me a hand hauling them over in a wheelbarrow and getting them into the fire. While we were working, I asked him if he'd heard any news about steps being taken to get things back under control and city services up and running again, but he seemed to be as in the dark as I am. The only thing he knew for sure was that roving gangs were on the loose and that we needed to be on the lookout because he'd heard some horror stories about the atrocities being committed by these groups.

I told them that just such a gang was responsible for the three dead in our courtyard and explained how it had gone down. He said he wasn't surprised. Then he told me about what he'd heard these gangs were doing. Turns out, if what he said was true, it sounds like it's worse out there than I thought.

Scott told me that he'd heard about a couple gangs hitting the other side of town and described the tactics they're using. The first such tactic involves using those in the early stages of the flu as

84

a sort of "zombie" infiltration unit to get into people's homes. Apparently, they send these flu carriers into a home at gunpoint. The person or people holding out inside the home are faced with a dilemma – either kill the "zombies" in self defense or, realizing that these people have the flu, kill them in an attempt to avoid being infected. Their only other option is to try to flee, at which point the gang of looters waiting outside will murder them. Then the gangs kill the "zombies" or force them on to infiltrate other targets while pillaging any remaining supplies in the home or building they just cleared.

The other tactic that Scott described is the one that concerns me most. He said that some of these gangs go looking specifically for families. They'll take several families captive and then they use the children or the wives as hostages. They force the younger more able family members to infiltrate the homes of people the gang suspect might have food or supplies. If the person or people refuse to act, the gang members kill one hostage at a time until those who remain finally submit to the gang's will. If the home is successfully infiltrated, the gang moves on to the next target, using the same tactic to get the remaining family members to work for them. If those family members fail in their home invasion, the gang kills the remaining hostages and finds new families to do its bidding. It's a win/win for the gangs, getting the supplies they need without risk to themselves. And it's a lose/lose for the families – if they succeeded in their raid, they are rewarded with another mission, and if they fail, the rest of their family dies brutally and sometimes sadistically at the hands of the gang members.

I was both glad and dismayed to have met up with Scott. His stories have scared the piss out of me and put me on guard more now than ever. If anything positive has come out of these revelations, it's that I'm going to fight tooth and nail to keep any and all intruders out of our home. In my opinion, it's better to go down fighting than be taken alive by such people.

With this knowledge, I quickly retreated to the relative safety of our condo building after loading the bodies of our fallen neighbors into the bonfire.

11:32 p.m.

I'm writing by the light of a single candle. Unfortunately, it looks like there were some unintended consequences of the Main Street bonfire. Like moths to a flame, it has drawn the looters back to our neighborhood. I saw a group of them go by just before it got dark and I just heard people down in the back alley. I could hear one of them trying our building's rear entry doors…thankfully without success. They then tried to get into a store across the alley from us. I heard them smashing one of the windows. I don't think they're going to find much, but I'm not going to be the one to tell them.

I've temporarily moved our refrigerator away from the kitchen window over in front of our kitchen's back door, and I've slid the hutch (that's very heavy since it's loaded with Kate's grandmother's old dishes) that typically sits in the central hallway over to block our front door. Before I did so, I offered to let the Williams' room with us for the night since they have no weapons with which to defend themselves should our stack of condo units be breached. They accepted. I also asked Ms. Murphy, but she graciously declined, saying that if she was going to die, she'd like to do so in the privacy of her own home. Good 'ol Ms. Murphy, stoic and steadfast as ever.

Now I'm on watch duty. Kate, Bradley, and Brenda are all still awake too. I gave the Williams' a crash course on gun use and safety in the event that the worst occurs.

It's been dark out for a while now, and fires are starting to pop up around town as these gangs of looters (or whatever you want to call them) start putting homes and businesses to the torch. You'd think they'd have better things to do…apparently not. I guess that when the rules of modern society have been taken away and the dogs are let loose, it's time to run wild. I think these people must just roam the city, taking what they want and doing what they want. I hear them running up and down the alley as I write this, yelling, screaming, shouting, shooting things, smashing things, and generally wreaking havoc and destruction on what was once our peaceful little village. It's frightening. I feel like it's only a matter of time before they focus on our building again.

Right now, it looks like they're hitting the large Victorian homes around us. Those houses don't stand a chance. They're big, they have big windows, many of the entry doors have large glass panes in them, and overall I can seem them being extremely tough structures to defend against intruders. A lot of them have security systems, but what good are those now? I feel for anyone left in those homes. I wonder how Scott, his neighbors, and their families are doing? There has to be close to 100 of these violent looters out there going crazy, maybe more. They're all armed and obviously have no compunction about using their weapons. It looks like any structure they want to get into, they'll get into. I can only pray for those citizens of our suburb who are still alive and trying to stay that way. Like suffering through the Su flu wasn't bad enough, now we've got to deal with this lawlessness and destruction from those left behind.

Saturday, September 14th

1:13 a.m.

I'm still writing by the light of my one lonely candle. I have to say, though, even this sole flame almost seems too bright on a night like tonight. Everyone is still awake – even the kids. We're all huddled in our living room, Brenda and Bradley Williams included. We've left the windows open so that we can hear what's going on outside, but I have drawn the shades to reduce the chances of anyone outside catching a glimpse of movement inside our unit. Poor Violet wants Kate to read to her, but I'm afraid to let them use more candles or a flashlight that might draw attention to our unit.

Things have gone from bad to worse outside as the night progresses. From our third-floor vantage point, I've counted at least ten fires burning around town. Gunfire has increased substantially, and it doesn't appear that the thugs or looters or gang bangers or whatever they are who have infiltrated our village are going anywhere soon.

I actually saw first hand out our living room windows what Scott told me about. It was hard to tell exactly what was happening since it was dark out and I only had the light of a burning house across the street to see by, but from what I could tell, a group of these invaders were forcing what appeared to be a group of area residents to conduct a home invasion. I could hear a lot of gunfire coming from around and inside the house, and then it went quiet. Several minutes later, the armed mob went inside the house. They made several trips back and forth, carrying out what I guess were supplies, before they torched the house.

After a few minutes, what I was afraid would happen, happened. The mob turned its attention to our condo building. Several of the armed gang tested the front gate. Finding it locked

(I re-secured it when I got back from hauling the corpses to the bonfire), they cut off the chain holding it closed with bolt cutters.

I was torn as to what to do. I didn't want them getting into the courtyard for fear of what happened to our neighbors several days ago, happening again. But I also didn't want to give away our location by firing warning shots. I was hoping that maybe these people would just leave if they thought the place was empty.

By the light of the growing house fire across from us, I could see that the intruders had gotten the gate open, and I knew I had to act. I made sure everyone was well away from the window, cracked the blinds slightly, and fired my .38 until it was out of bullets. I tried aiming at the flowerbeds around the gate since I have absolutely no desire to kill anyone even if they aren't the nicest people in the world. Plus, since I couldn't see the faces of the people outside, I wasn't sure if the people trying to gain access to our courtyard were possibly friends and neighbors from our community who had been put up to this by having their own loved ones held hostage.

The shots I fired were extremely loud, and their sound reverberated intensely inside our living room. Poor Violet was left weeping quietly and shaking violently when I'd finished, but the gunfire seemed to have the intended effect as the group clustered around the gate beat a hasty retreat.

It now looks like the multitude of thugs and criminals invading our community have moved down the street in search of easier pickings, but I've reloaded my gun just in case and the shotgun's within reach. It felt weird to fire the gun again, especially when it was aimed toward actual people, not at the gun range.

I wish these people would find something else to do and move on...but move on to what? Where do they have to go? What else do they have to do?

Is this how our world's going to be?

Unfortunately, I guess so. Things are getting worse, not better. I'm not sure what to do. Right now, it's just about surviving to see another day. But then what? What happens a couple weeks from now when the food runs out? What happens if society as we once knew it never returns? What do WE do? Where do WE go? Will the world be taken over by the kind of people roaming our community – people who don't play by the rules…who apparently HAVE no rules?

It's frightening enough for us adults, but what about poor Dylan and Violet? What do they have to look forward to in that sort of environment?

Maybe we can get out of the city. Maybe things are better in small towns where communities were tighter knit before the flu. We've kind of missed our chance, but if we can wait things out until these groups have picked places clean – or at least THINK they've picked them clean – maybe we can take a shot at getting out of town. The bad thing (ONE of the bad things) is that we'll probably have to attempt our escape on foot since trying to drive out of the city would only call more attention to ourselves from people like those outside right now.

But how long do we wait? A week? Two weeks? A month? Will we have enough food and water to survive that long, especially when having to supplement our neighbors? Do we try to take them along? There's no way we can take Ms. Murphy. She'd never make such a trek. She's too old. And she'd probably never agree to leave her home anyway. So what do we do, just leave her here to die?

These are horrible questions, and right now, I'm not finding any answers.

Oh no, I hear people again outside.

6:14 a.m.

I'm writing this as the early-morning sky begins to brighten. I got very little sleep last night. Hardly any of us did. None of us ate well last night either, but no one seems to be hungry.

The gunfire and number of structures burning around us have continued to grow throughout the pre-dawn hours, and unlike before, the people responsible for wreaking such havoc did not recede into the shadows come daybreak. In fact, it seems like things outside have gotten worse, and continue to grow worse (if that's even possible) as I write this.

Bullets have been hitting the side of our building all night long. We continually hear the thumps, thuds, zips, and zings of various impacts with our building's brick façade interspersed with the occasional crack or crash of glass as a round comes in through a window. We crawl on our hands and knees whenever one of us has to use the bathroom, and we always make it a quick trip, ensuring that we keep our heads down.

Poor Violet has been crying almost non-stop throughout the night. She's absolutely terrified.

Kate and I keep telling both her and Dylan that it's going to be okay, but it's hard to sound convincing with the amount of gunfire and structural fires raging around us. I wish these animals outside would just take their loot and go, but it's almost like they want more than just stuff. It's as though they're rabid beasts that are wild with bloodlust. They want to shoot, to kill, and to destroy just for the thrill of it, just because they have nothing better to do and they have the opportunity to exercise their destructive prowess without restraint…just because they CAN. At this point, I'd be willing to give them everything we have if they'd just go away, but I know that wouldn't end it. They'd take us prisoner and use us to do their bidding or just kill us outright.

I'm going to make a quick trip downstairs to check on Ms. Murphy as soon as it's totally light outside. I'm going to take her some food and water – enough for the entire day so that I don't have to make another trip. With the bullets flying the way they are, it's not worth taking chances, although with the exception of the skylight at its top, the main stairwell of our condo stack is probably one of the safest and most secure spots in our entire building due to its interior location. If things get too bad, we might be forced to relocate there for tonight to reduce the chances of being struck by a stray bullet or someone seeing us.

7:47 a.m.

Ms. Murphy is no longer with us.

I went down to her unit about 10 minutes ago during a slight lull in the shooting outside. I found the poor gal in her rocking chair, set before the living room window. She'd been shot

91

in head. There was a bullet hole in the window. I'm guessing that the stubborn woman just wouldn't hear what I was telling her about staying away from the windows. She probably wanted to let Felix watch his birds this morning and decided these assholes outside weren't going to deter them from their regular routine. Then, either someone saw her moving through the window or it was a ricochet or a bullet fired haphazardly that just happened to have her name on it.

There was an open jar of green olives (the same jar I had brought down to her the other day) set on the table beside her rocking chair. I'm guessing that she was feeding Felix his treats while they watched the birds. Poor thing. She didn't deserve this. I guess none of us deserve this, but it's what we got.

As much as it pains me to say it, Ms. Murphy's passing does unburden me from one of those nagging questions I'd been asking myself earlier. Now I don't have to worry about what to do with her should we try to escape the Chicagoland area. However, I find myself now being straddled with new responsibilities. I have to deal with Ms. Murphy's remains.

While I was in her condo, I pulled the comforter from her bed and laid it out on the living room floor. Then I lifted her amazingly light body from the rocking chair and bound her inside the blanket. I'll deal with taking her outside later, hopefully once things calm down.

I also found Felix. He was hiding under her bed. Using a few olives, I was able to coax him out and into his cat carrier that I discovered in the bedroom closet. I brought him and his cat box up to our condo. The old fellow is currently sniffing around, exploring his new digs. Dylan and Violet are super excited to have him here. I hope he will be a nice distraction in what otherwise has become a very shitty situation for them. Other than a few gold fish that died last year, they've never had a real pet, and it makes me feel good to see them happy again. I still need to go back downstairs and get the rest of Felix's cat litter, but I think I'll save that for later.

Right now, I'm going to cook up one of our cans of corned beef hash to go with our cereal this morning. We haven't had much meat lately, and I think everyone is craving a little protein in their diet.

I find it somewhat hard to believe I'm thinking about food at a time like this. I just dealt with the dead body of one of our neighbors. Sadly, I think I'm beginning to become hardened to this new life and way of living.

We're starting to run into another issue now that we've been without utility services for some time now – clean clothes. Because we've been unable to shower regularly, and we've been left to the whim of the warm summer temperatures, our clothing (especially socks and underwear) are becoming soiled faster than normal. I'm not sure exactly what we're going to do about it. I guess we could take some of the water we drained from our hot water tank, fill a couple buckets like we do for our bathing, and wash our clothes. We can open the window and hang them up to dry in the kitchen once things calm down outside. But I really don't want to use our valuable water resources for such non-essential purposes. I've asked everyone to try to extend their clothing wear for as long as possible, but at some point, we're going to have to break down and wash at least some socks and underwear once we run out of clean replacements. For right now, we're left just putting the worst of our soiled items into several big garbage bags that we keep tied shut.

And now I'm off to play chef for the family (and Brenda and Bradley). Dylan and Violet want to help me since they're going bat-shit crazy looking for things to do, but I think I'll leave them to play with Felix. It's not much, but I'm willing to give about anything a chance to distract them from what's going on outside. We've been doing our best to find activities to take their minds off things, but it's kind of hard to concentrate when the world is falling apart around you.

11:03 a.m.

Something is going on outside. I can't tell exactly what it is, but it's occurring on the other side of the building. We heard a large bang over there a few minutes ago, and now we can see smoke rising from the alley on that side of the building. There's also some smoke starting to filter out the broken window of a third floor unit across the courtyard from us. This is very disconcerting because if a fire has started over there, it could spread and threaten to consume the entire building. I really don't want to go over there, but I can't see that I have much of a choice. If I don't, we could face being burned out of our home and lose not just our safe haven but all our supplies. Plus, then where will we go? We'll be forced into the midst of the chaos currently swirling around us.

12:14 p.m.

Kate is working on my leg as I write this. I'll try to provide a brief rundown of what I just went through while she cleans and bandages my injuries. Hopefully the writing will help keep my mind off the pain.

After seeing the smoke coming from third-floor unit across the courtyard from us, I decided I needed to put out any potential fire brewing within. I grabbed the small fire extinguisher from under our kitchen sink, got my .38 (that I'm now keeping on top of the bookshelf in our main corridor so that it's away from the kids but readily available), and gave Bradley the loaded shotgun. I told him to cover me from the window and explained that I was going to make a mad dash from our front entrance, out across the courtyard, and over to the front entrance of the stack that contained the smoking unit. There, I planned to shoot through the glass entry door, make my way upstairs, and hopefully put out the fire. Writing it down now on paper, it looks like a pretty piss-poor plan, so I'm not surprised it didn't work.

The first obstacle I encountered was our stairwell entry door that I'd covered with plywood. I had Kate come down and help me temporarily unseal it. After we got the plywood off, I sent Kate back upstairs to barricade herself and the rest of the family inside our condo.

The next problem I came up against was making it unnoticed across the courtyard and to the other side of the building. After unlocking our foyer door, I hadn't taken more than a few steps outside before I was met with gunfire from the street. I heard Bradley fire the shotgun, but it was no use. The shooting from the street kept up, stopping my progress and driving me back inside our entry foyer.

Once inside, I quickly relocked the foyer door and made my way back to the stairwell. Kate hadn't even made it all the way upstairs by the time I'd returned, so she came back down and helped me get the piece of plywood screwed back in place.

I was then faced with finding a new way to get over to that side of the building. It was then that it hit me – the roof access.

I feel like such an idiot now. I should have thought of it first thing. The roof access is comprised of a steel rung ladder built into the bricks that form one wall of our rear stairwell. The ladder is found almost directly outside our back door. It leads to an unlocked hatch in the ceiling with have access to the entire rooftop that is completely flat.

Kate and I headed back upstairs where Brenda (who we'd left to watch the kids) and Bradley let us back inside the condo. Once back inside, Dylan helped me hurriedly un-barricaded the rear door while Kate, Brenda, and Bradley re-barricaded the front. I was up on the roof in probably less than two minutes. The hardest part of climbing up the steel-rung ladder was hauling the fire extinguisher along with me. I had to pull myself up the ladder with one hand while holding the fire extinguisher with the other. At the top of the ladder, I had to balance the extinguisher on the rung I was standing on, leaning it against the wall, while I unlatched the roof access hatch and pushed it open.

Once I was on the rooftop, I did a crouched run across the back end of our building and around to the street-facing tip of our U-shaped structure. There, I had to figure out a way back inside the building. My first thought was to climb down the side of the building and go in through a window. But I figured that could be time consuming and dangerous, plus, I would expose myself to gunfire from the street. It was then that I noticed the central stairwell skylight belonging to this particular stack of condo units. I made my way over to the skylight and peeked down through the glass to make sure no one was beneath it in the stairwell below. There was smoke in the stairwell but not so much that I couldn't see. Other than that, it appeared empty. At first, I tried to break the skylight's glass with the fire extinguisher. But after a few failed attempts at bashing it, I quickly realized the glass was harder to smash than I anticipated. It was then that I thought of the .38 pistol I had shoved into my waistband while climbing to the roof.

OUCH! Oh man, that really hurt. Kate just dabbed at the cut on my leg with an alcohol-soaked cotton ball. I haven't felt pain like that since I broke my leg playing high school football.

Anyway, back to the skylight. Before I did anything else, I went to the building's edge and checked the alley by the trash receptacles. It looked as though someone had blasted open one of the entry doors to the building. The area around the door was still smoldering. But otherwise, the alley was devoid of people. I was hoping that this meant the interior of this portion of the building was clear as well, but I wasn't taking it for granted. I then hustled back to the skylight where I aimed my gun, pulled the trigger once, then moved my aim about a foot to the right of the first bullet impact and squeezed off another round. The rounds passed easily through, cracking the glass but not shattering it. Then I stuck the gun back in my waistband, picked up the fire extinguisher, and used it to smash out the skylight's glass. With the skylight clear, I dropped the fire extinguisher through the open hole. It landed with a heavy thud on the stairwell landing below. I landed with a thud just beside it, but that's not how I hurt my leg. In fact, I was feeling pretty pleased with myself by this point in my little adventure. I'd gotten to the site of the fire unnoticed and successfully made my way back inside the building. And I had the means to fight whatever was burning with a larger fire extinguisher that I had commandeered from the stairwell wall.

The door to the unit with the suspected fire was closed. I could see dark gray smoke seeping from around it, but I remained confident. It wasn't until I entered the unit – the door to which was unlocked – my .38 in one hand, a fire extinguisher in the other, that I realized my folly. I had assumed that since something was burning inside, the unit would be devoid of people.

It wasn't.

As soon as I entered the condo's living room, I saw a couch smoldering against the far wall. It was the only thing that was burning. But it wasn't the smoking couch that grabbed my attention as much as the person coming toward me from the kitchen. He looked to be in his mid-20s and was carrying a cardboard box that was filled with canned goods. At first, I thought it was the unit owner, but the automatic rifle slung over his shoulder said otherwise.

We both stopped dead in our tracks, me in the center of the living room, him near the exit of the kitchen about 15 feet from me. We eyed each other for a fraction of a second before we each went for our weapons. He made the first move, but it took him longer because he was still holding the box of food. He also had to maneuver his gun, which was slung part way around his back, around in front of him, get a grip on it, and fire. He tried doing this while at the same time not dropping the box of supplies he held. Meanwhile I already had my .38 out and in hand.

I only fired twice because I'd already used two bullets to shoot out the skylight and just had four left in the gun. One of my shots went wide, but the other one hit the guy in the arm, causing him to fumble his assault rifle. Apparently it did enough damage so that he gave up any further attempt at firing back at me. Instead, he threw the box of food at me. It hit me in the chest causing me to drop the fire extinguisher as I tried to half catch, half block it. Meanwhile, the guy made a break for it, bolting past me and through the front door. There was no way I was going to go after him. I was just relieved to see him disappear into the hallway and down the front stairs.

With the intruder gone, I recovered the fire extinguisher and quickly put out the smoldering sofa. Once the fire was out, I had no desire to remain in the unit any longer than necessary. I briefly contemplated gathering the box of food that the guy had thrown at me. But I was afraid that if he or any of the people that might be with him came back for the items and found them missing, rather than just taking them and leaving, they'd instead come looking for whoever had removed them – ME! Therefore, I left them there.

I then realized the new dilemma facing me – how to safely get out of the stack of condo units I was in and back to my own. I certainly didn't want to follow the guy I'd shot, since not only might I meet up with him again, but I'd have to cross the courtyard. Plus, even if I did make it back across the courtyard without being shot, I'd be locked out of my own unit stack and would have to break through the barriers I'd put in place. Otherwise, I had the option of going down the rear stairway, but that would lead me out to the exposed side alley. Then I'd have to go around to the alley behind our building to get to our own stack's rear entrance. And even though I hadn't seen anyone down there, it didn't mean they weren't lurking somewhere. This left me with what I felt was my best option – going back up and out the skylight through which I'd entered. The problem was, the skylight was a good 12 feet above the stairwell landing. It wasn't hard to drop down through it, but getting back up and out of it was another story. However, after some quick thinking, I came up with a plan.

I pushed a desk inside the unit out into the hallway. It wasn't high enough to get me as far up as I needed to be to climb through the skylight, so I got a wooden chair and put it on top. This was my error. The chair wasn't as balanced as I thought, and it kicked out from under me as I reached for the skylight opening. I landed awkwardly on the stairwell landing, right on top of the toppled chair, smashing it. In so doing, part of the jagged broken chair stabbed me in the leg like a spear.

While it was a bad injury, it wasn't so debilitating that I couldn't re-attempt my escape. This time around, I found a sturdier, more stable step stool that gave me the elevation I needed to pull myself up through the skylight and make it (albeit limping badly) back down to our condo.

And now, Kate has my leg cleaned and wrapped. She put plenty of antibiotic ointment on it to reduce the chance of it getting infected. With the way things are now, and not having the ability to get medical attention or even see a doctor, the last thing I need is an infection. In this sort of environment, I now realize that even a simple scratch, left without proper care, could be a death sentence. Violet is sitting here with me, holding my free hand while I write (little sweetheart, she's so worried about her Daddy).

Alright, I'm off to have a drink or two, not just to dull the pain, but to calm my nerves after having shot someone (that's a first). I also want to grab something to eat and to say a prayer of thanks for getting through all that mess relatively safely. Then I need to clean and reload the guns. I'm down to 18 rounds for the .38. I hope I don't need them, but the way things are going, I'm damn glad I have them.

1:48 p.m.

We ate packages of Ramen noodles for lunch, largely because they're quick, easy, and fill us up. I had two warm beers and a couple aspirin with my meal to help calm me down and ease the pain of my leg injury. I find myself kind of wishing I had a pack of cigarettes. I'm not a smoker (except occasionally when I'm having a cocktail), but I could sure go for a cigarette right about now.

Everyone is pretty quiet. There's not much to talk about, and what we CAN talk about, we don't WANT to talk about. I'm really proud of the family though. They're handling this like real troopers. Kate's staying strong, the kids aren't complaining (too much), and I feel as though we're tighter now than ever before. I know everyone is scared, but they're all doing their best to put on brave faces.

I hate that the kids have to go through this. I hate that ALL of us have to go through it, but especially the kids. No kid should have their childhood innocence torn asunder by something this tragic and traumatic. I wonder if things will ever get back to normal for them…for *any* of us.

After we finished eating, Brenda and Bradley went back to their condo across the hall to have a little privacy. They took a two-gallon bucket with them to fill from their unit's water heater so that they can clean up and use the bathroom.

I think these roving gangs (although I'm not exactly sure if they are multiple gangs or just one large one) have set up camp in our once cozy and secure village. I have a feeling that they just go suburb to suburb bleeding each area dry of its resources, destroying them as they do so. It's kind of weird…ironic, I guess. It reminds me of the Su flu itself. I remember seeing in the news reports – back when we were still getting news reports – about how the flu is systemic. It circulates through the body shutting down organ after organ until the body can no longer function or defend itself. While I can't say for sure, I'm willing to bet that this is what's happening all across the Chicagoland area. These types of gangs are probably going suburb by suburb shutting them down, slowly dismantling what's left of the city piece by piece. The Su flu starts the collapse of civilization and then leaves it up to the societal remnants to finish the job.

I wonder if anyone will survive all this? If they do, what will they turn the world into in a year, two years, ten years from now? The prospects are terrifying to say the least. I can't live this way. Well, I guess I shouldn't say that. I CAN live this way, but I don't WANT to live this way. And I DEFINITELY don't want my children to have to live this way.

Uh oh, I hear something next door in the Williams' condo. Sounds like loud banging. I'd better go see what's up. I really don't want to. God I'm exhausted. I just want to be left alone. Is that really too much to ask?

3:11 p.m.

I guess being "left alone" IS too much to ask, but again, the irony of the situation strikes me hard as I write it. We're just as alone now as when we began this whole mess. First, it was Ms. Laurel downstairs, then it was Ms. Murphy, and now it's Brenda and Bradley Williams who are dead. It's all just too much. I hope that one day I can look back on these pages and remember what we suffered through and appreciate how much better we have it, but I'm beginning to wonder if that day will ever come.

And while I really don't want to rehash what just happened to our neighbors – our FRIENDS – I'm going to. I owe it to them to tell their story and not have them be forgotten in the hellish hole our world now seems to have become.

I probably should have seen something like this happening, but hindsight is always 20/20. The exposed stairwells appears to be our building's Achilles' Heel. It's how people got into the unit with the smoldering sofa, and it must be how people got into the Williams' unit.

The steel cages that enclose these stairwells that exit into the alleys running alongside our U-shaped building don't extend all the way up. In fact, they only extend up about 15 feet. So even with the steel cage doors having self-locking mechanisms, someone could scale the metal grating and enter the stairwell around the second floor.

Unfortunately, there's not much I can do about this weak point in our structure. There are four such exposed stairwells, two on each side of the building. There's no way to block them once the top of the cage ends. Of course, I guess I could dismantle portions of the wood steps and landings, but it would take forever, and doing so would likely only draw more unwanted attention to our building.

The banging sounds I heard at the end of my last entry must have been the intruders breaking down the Williams' back door. Unfortunately, we hadn't taken the precautions with their unit that we had with our own (although now we have moved the unit's refrigerator in front of the smashed back door and wedged it in place with a large cushion chair).

Once the intruders were inside the unit, it didn't take them long to find Brenda and Bradley. The particular unit in question is a small one bedroom. Brenda was in the bathroom when the intruders entered – they apparently killed her first since they would have found her before they found Bradley as they came in through the kitchen. Since the home invaders had entered through the back, it made it harder for me to get inside when I heard the commotion. Brenda had locked the front door to the condo (the door facing our unit) after they left our place. This meant that they were safer from intruders entering from this direction, but it also meant that they were left exposed and defenseless when I tried to come to their rescue since I couldn't get into the condo quickly.

After trying the front door and finding it locked, I quickly went back to our own unit and got the shotgun. Not knowing the situation awaiting me within the other condo, I wanted as much firepower with me as possible. Unfortunately, those critical seconds may have meant the difference between life and death for poor Bradley. When I was back in our own unit, I heard several more shots, which I'm guessing was Bradley being killed.

Just as I got back to the Williams' unit, the front door opened. I was confronted by a guy wearing a blue bandana over his face and a black ball cap. I think we were both surprised to find ourselves face to face with one another. He was carrying a handgun and began to raise it as soon as he saw me. Then he hesitated slightly. This gave me the chance I needed. I had no choice – I shot him. Thank God Dad's old shotgun didn't malfunction. Pellets ripped into the guy and spackled the door and walls around him. I think he was dead before he hit the floor.

God that's weird to see in print. It was bad enough having to wound somebody when I shot the guy in the arm earlier in the day. But killing someone is an altogether different feeling. Between the overwhelming sense of guilt and feeling like I'm some sort of criminal, I can already tell it's something that's going to weigh on me for the rest of my life. I know I did what I had to do to protect myself and my family, but I still feel like it was wrong. It frightens me writing down that I killed a man. Will I be prosecuted after all this is done? Will I have to claim self defense? Jeez, the shooting didn't even occur in my own home. That will look bad to a jury. Maybe they'll say that the guy had a right to be in our building. Maybe they'll say that he could have thought that *I* was the intruder and that HE could have been firing in self defense.

What am I saying? There won't be any courtrooms, trials or juries after all this is done with. There probably won't be enough people to even FILL a jury. But God is always watching. How will I be judged in that respect? A life is a life, and I just took one. Justified or not, it has to be viewed as wrong in the eyes of God. There may have been a better way to deal with the situation. Maybe I could have talked to the guy. Yeah, and then maybe I'D be the one laying on the landing outside, along with the rest of my family. I guess there's no definitive answer. It is what it is…and it SUCKS!

So back to what happened inside the Williams' unit. The blast from the shotgun must have scared anyone else who may have been inside, because by the time I made my way around the guy I'd shot and through the front door, the unit was empty. As I got to the rear door, I saw two more dudes fleeing down the back stairs and out into the alley. I fired at them with the shotgun. I think I hit one partially in the shoulder, but at that distance, it didn't do much damage. It was more of a warning to them not to come back. They both escaped down the side alley, and disappeared around the front of the building.

After checking on Brenda and Bradley, and finding them both dead, I made a quick trip back to our condo to let Kate and the kids know that I was okay but for the kids to stay put. Then Kate came back with me and helped moved the fridge and chair to block the back door of the Williams' condo.

By the time we finished with our work and got back to our own unit, three buildings (one beside us and two across the back alley from us) were on fire. They're stores with easily accessible ground levels, but that does little to ease my mind about our own situation. If these people can get in through the less secure alley stairways, it's only a matter of time before they find their way to our condo. They could get in through one of the lower level units and then come up our front stairs. I can't watch everywhere at once. And there are plenty of windows as well as the skylights that are options for getting into the building if people really want to, and apparently people REALLY want to. I think the best thing to do right now is to just stay put and just hope that people get into enough other units and take enough stuff from them that they think they've got it all. And hopefully they'll find our unit secure enough and dangerous enough (with me being armed) that they'll just leave us alone and move on to easier pickings.

Maybe it's heartless to say – at least I FEEL heartless saying it – but I almost feel safer now that it's just me, Kate, and the kids. Having other people around only seemed to make our situation more difficult and more dangerous. Now, all I have to focus on is protecting us, which brings me to our plan.   Kate doesn't particularly like it, but tough shit. With the way things are now, we've got to do what we've got to do to protect the kids…and that's it, no questions asked.

So here it is.

If someone tries coming in the front door, Kate is to take the kids down the back stairs to the basement storage area while I attempt to hold off the intruders. We considered going to the rooftop, but with the access ladder just outside our back door, it seemed too obvious. Once downstairs, Kate will hide herself and the kids in a gap that we created (after the whole Williams' debacle) behind a bunch of boxes in our storage unit. This cave is small, but once inside, the entry crawlspace can be covered with a box so that it's not visible to anyone from outside. It is surrounded by other storage units full of stuff and it would take some time for anyone searching the space to uncover. The exterior walls of these storage units are formed from chicken wire, so people will easily be able to see and hear inside them. I consider this both a good and bad thing. Since anyone making a search of the area will be able to see inside the cages, they may not spend much time actually trying to get into them. However, it also means Kate and the kids will have to be very careful. The smallest noise could give away their position. We had a talk with the kids – especially Violet – about being as still and as quiet as possible should they need to take shelter there. We did our best to explain to them that it is literally a matter of life and death. I think that at this point, they get it.

Should intruders make it up through the rear stairwell, our plan is for me to hold them off long enough for Kate and the kids to make their way out the front door and across to the Williams' unit. There, they will split up, Kate and Violet hiding under the bed that we moved from downstairs while Dylan hides in the furnace closet in a small gap behind the hot water heater. Not to be crude, but we're going to leave Brenda and Bradley's bodies where they fell for the time being. I'm also leaving the dead guy in the hallway. That way, any outsiders entering the condo will not only find it devoid of food and supplies, but they'll find dead bodies. It will hopefully move them along quicker and make them think that the place has already been raided and picked clean.

In either situation, I'll stay behind with the shotgun to defend our condo. In the process, this will make it look like it was just me holing up inside. Kate doesn't like this last part of our plan, as it doesn't give me great chances of surviving, but we have to make it look good. It doesn't make sense for a buttoned up condo full of supplies like ours to be devoid of occupants should someone break in. That means that intruders might search for us, finding us ALL rather than just finding me. Kate wants to know what I'll do after I make a show of force. It's a good question. I'm not really sure. I told her that we probably won't have to execute the plan, that these outsiders are bound to move on soon. They've spent enough time here. There can't be much left to take. I'm hoping they're like locust, coming in a swarm, ravaging a spot, and then quickly moving on. I just wish they'd go...God how I wish they'd go. It'd make an already incredibly difficult situation just a little bit easier.

3:39 p.m.

Someone's down in the street with a megaphone. They're shouting something up at the building, but I can't make out exactly what they're saying. Dylan's got the binoculars out. He says the guy with the megaphone has a woman with him and a kid that looks like his friend, Liam. I'm going to see if I can hear what the guy is yelling about.

104

3:49 p.m.

Dear God, what have I done? The man I killed was Scott, the father of Dylan's friend, Liam. I had no idea. It all happened so fast, and he was wearing that hat and bandana. He's never been to our condo before, so he probably had no idea that this was our place. The people trying to get into our building must have sent him in to clear the place in one of those forced home-invasion teams he was telling me about. I guess he knew what he was talking about.

The dude on the street was yelling for Scott to come back out, obviously not knowing that he was already dead by my hand. The guy, and the group that was with him, were threatening Scott's wife. They said that unless he came out in one minute, they were going to kill her. They counted down and then shot her right there on the street. It was the longest minute of my life. I wanted to do something, shout to them that he was dead, but I knew it wouldn't matter. They were going to kill her anyway. At least that's what I keep telling myself now. And by answering them, I'd only be giving away our own position, potentially risking the lives of my own family.

After the guy shot Scott's wife, he did the same thing with Dylan's friend, Liam. By that point, I couldn't even watch. I closed the window and made sure the blinds were down so that the kids wouldn't see. Dylan kept asking me what was going on. I lied and told him that the people had left. There is no way I can tell him the truth. It's all too horrible. I keep telling myself that it's not my fault, that their having been captured meant that this would have happened to them sooner or later. But having pulled the trigger that killed Scott leaves me personally shouldering this terrible burden of responsibility.

4:43 p.m.

There is a big firefight going on out front. A bunch of dudes in SUVs and pickup trucks just arrived and they're letting the guys who killed Scott's family have it. Could it be that the cavalry has finally arrived? Maybe this is some sort of new National Guard, a kind of local militia formed by area citizens to

combat the roving gangs and renegades. I pray to God that it is.
This could be our salvation.

5:39 p.m.

These people are definitely NOT our salvation. They drove
vehicles in through our front gate, threw a grenade into one of our
lower floor windows, and are generally blowing our building to
shit!

We're all hunkered in our condo's central hallway…the
best spot we could find to protect us from what's going on. There
are a lot of armed personnel and they're all over the place outside.
I told Kate and the kids to be ready to move at a moment's notice.
We've gathered a backpack for each of us – a "bug-out bag" so to
speak – to take along in the event we have to leave quickly and
can't make it back to the condo. Each pack has four bottled
waters, three packs of Ramen noodles (since they're light and
durable), a small freezer bag of cereal, and a bag of cookies. In
addition, Dylan's pack has a can of corned beef, a container of
crackers, two cans of beans, and two cans of fruit cocktail. Kate's
pack has a flashlight, the .38 (along with the rest of the ammo), a
jar of peanut butter, two cans of beans, two cans of oranges, a can
opener, and some silverware. It's not much, but it will give us a
couple day's rations should we need it.

I pray we don't. We all do.

My pack has a few medical supplies, a couple additional
bottles of water, some extra cans of fruit, more cereal, some packs
of fruit chews, and a water bottle full of vodka (for trade or wound
cleansing).

I hear banging downstairs and glass shattering. Sounds like
they've broken into the entry foyer and are now working on the
plywood covering over the front stairwell door. It's time to go.
I'll kiss the family goodbye and send them to un-barricade the
back door. Then I'll wait at the front door with the shogun. Violet
and Dylan are crying. Now Kate is too. Hell, I'm even crying.
Saying goodbye to them is the toughest thing I've ever had to do,
but it's worth it if there's a chance it'll keep them alive.

Okay, deep breath…this is it.

<u>Epilogue</u>

"You might want to check this out," Eight Ball gave a nod as he offered the book to his boss.

"What the fuck is it?" his boss eyeballed him with an angry, almost challenging stare.

"Looks like a journal or somethin'. Pulled it off the guy we killed getting in here."

"Yeah?" his boss shrugged. "So fuckin' what? I care about some diary this guy was keeping all his fuckin' hopes and dreams in? What, he's a fucking little girl or something?"

Eight Ball shrugged, "Thought it might be important." He leafed through the book. "Thought maybe it'd tell us somethin'."

"Tell us *what!?*" his boss almost shouted. "How he fuckin' brushed his hair before bed each night? Who he had a fuckin' crush on in the sixth grade? Jesus, you're a fuckin' dumbass, Eight Ball. I don't know why I keep you around."

Eight Ball stared at the floor bashfully, ashamed, embarrassed by the berating. He was just trying to please his boss. He thought there might be something useful in the book. It must have been kind of important for the guy living here to still have it on him when he died. He continued to leaf through the book. As he did so, an envelope fell from within.

"What the fuck's that?" Eight Ball's boss nodded to the envelope that had landed near Eight Ball's feet.

Eight Ball bent, picked it up, and pulled several sheets of paper from within.

"Give me that!" his boss commanded.

Eight Ball dutifully handed over the envelope.

"The goddamn papers too, you fuckin' moron!" his boss barked.

"Uh huh," Eight Ball grunted, handing over the papers.

"Christ," his boss swore. "Go make yourself useful!" he spat.

"Doin' what?" Eight Ball mumbled.

"Fuck do I care!? Go find the rest of these assholes…this guy's fucking family! They've got to be around here somewhere."

"Maybe they're dead," Eight Ball said.

"Won't know unless you fuckin' look, will you?" his boss gave him a death stare. "So get on it…we've got to make examples of people like this. Can't let them hole up like this, kill three of our guys, and then escape. Have to get in and kill 'em all. That way people will fear us. All we'll have to do is show up and they'll be scrambling to give us whatever the fuck we want. Gotta make a name for ourselves. This is a new fuckin' world. *Our fuckin' world!"*

Eight Ball nodded slowly. He thought he understood what his boss was saying, but he wasn't sure. He gathered a couple more members of their crew to help him search the rest of the building. On his way out the back door, he tossed the journal he'd found on the kitchen counter.

After Eight Ball left, his boss sat down on a nearby sofa with the letter. He took a slug from the open tequila bottle he carried with him and then began to read the letter to himself.

It read as follows:

August 24th

    Dear Chris and Kate,

    I hope this letter finds you and the kids well. It seems like forever since we saw you last. I bet Violet and Dylan are growing like weeds. Can you believe that Jason is already two and cruising briskly toward three? I'd like for us to get together for his birthday, if not sooner, which brings me to my point for writing.

    To jump right to the heart of the matter, I'm not sure how much you've been paying attention to all this Su flu stuff that's been on the news lately. I know it probably just seems like another one of those "chicken little" scenarios – SARS, Bird flu, Swine flu, Ebola, and the like. I'll admit, the sky seems like it's about to fall every time we turn on the nightly news. But I think it's more than that this time.

    While you might be aware that I've had a long-time interest in the outdoors, I'm not sure you know the full extent of the steps

I've taken to prepare for an emergency scenario. Whether it's a storm, power outage, pandemic or similar event, I've set some food and supplies aside to ensure the family is secure. And I've taken that planning a bit further lately with the appearance of the Su flu. No, I'm not one of those over-the-top preppers who is digging his own bunker in the backyard or has three years worth of food stashed away in five-gallon buckets, but I like having a plan should something go wrong.

I've recently contacted Claire's father about taking a trip down to a plot of land in southern Illinois around the Shawnee National Forest. The place belongs to a friend of his who said we could utilize the spot for camping. I'm taking Claire and Jason there over Labor Day weekend and I'd like to invite your family to join us. I'm sending a similar letter to other close friends and family members. It would make for good practice for getting out of the city in an emergency and seeing what living "off the grid" is like. If the Su flu turns out to be as bad as I think it might be, such a trip could also put us ahead of the curve. But even if you think I'm a little nuts for writing this (and I wouldn't blame you), such a trip with the family could turn out to be a lot of fun and give everyone a chance to get away from the city for a few days – a family retreat of sorts.

Please consider what I've said, and if you're up for it, pack a few bags, bring your supplies (the more the better), and meet us down in southern Illinois. Hope to see you soon!

John Stevens

P.S. – I've included a map and directions to get to our camp location. Don't feel obligated to call ahead, just come. We'd love to see you!

"Hmph," Eight Ball's boss snorted, folding the letter and the map crudely and jamming them roughly back inside the envelope. He took another swig of tequila.

A beautiful Latina sauntered in through the condo's front door. She slinked over to stand a few feet from the man sitting on the sofa. He was still holding the envelope.

"Change of plans," he said to her after a moment of silence between them.

"What's up now?" she asked, feeling a mixture of exasperation, intrigue, and anticipation for what this odd character she'd hooked up with was tossing her way this time. She both loved and hated the fact that he was willing and extremely capable of changing course right in the middle of a plan that seemed to her to be working quite well.

The guy half grinned, half sneered at her, almost as though he was welcoming her to challenge him. But she didn't.

"What have you got up your sleeve this time, Jake Stines?" she smirked at him with an evil sexiness.

"Get your sweet ass over here, Ava," he grinned, motioning her over.

She moved closer. He stood and wrapped an arm around her waist, giving her taut rear a smack.

"We're heading south," he told her with an unwavering confidence she found irresistibly macho.

"Where to?" she asked, nuzzling in closer so that her firm breasts were shoved up hard against him.

"Gonna try our hand in southern Illinois," he showed her the map.

"What's in southern Illinois?" Ava asked, tooling a finger across Jake's shoulder and down around his chest.

"Not sure," Jake said, opening the map and showing it to her. "Sounds like the guy we killed in this condo had people down there…people with a camp and supplies. I'm thinking we go down there, hitting smaller towns along the way. Should be easy pickings. Then we hit their camp, take their shit, and move on. Maybe we'll land in Memphis and take a look around there. Chicago's getting played out. Too much competition for what's left. Here, we're small fish in a big pond. We roll in and hit these little spots though, and then we're big fish in a little pond. Get my drift?"

Ava got it. She didn't totally agree with Jake that rural spots would be easy pickings, but she saw some merit in the idea. And she definitely liked the thought of heading south…back toward home.

Eight Ball slid shadowlike into the room, back from his search of the building. "Didn't find anybody," he told his boss.

"You looked everywhere?" Jake didn't even glance up from the map that he and Ava were still studying.

"Everywhere," Eight Ball nodded.

"The roof? I saw an access in the back stairwell."

"Yup. Nothin'."

"Basement?"

"Just storage…bunch of boxes, Christmas decorations, empty luggage, that sort of stuff."

Jake finally looked away from the map and over toward the men finishing up their work in the rest of the condo. They were carrying the last few boxes of supplies downstairs to be loaded into their vehicles before they moved on. Most of Jake's men were already downstairs congregating around their vehicles. They smoked cigarettes, ate, drank, and waited for their fearless leader to guide them to their next destination and to their next set of victims.

Ava started to move away but Jake grabbed, pulling her up close and kissing her hard before releasing her.

She again turned to leave. He watched her as she went, enjoying the view as she exited the living room and headed out the front door. He listened to the sound of her footsteps fade as she descended the staircase.

Once Ava was gone, Jake re-folded the map and letter and put them back inside the envelope.

"Here," he said, handing the envelope to Eight Ball. "Hold onto this, and get the rest of the crew ready. We roll in five."

Eight Ball nodded his understanding of the command and hurried downstairs.

Jake took a deep breath and another long drink of his tequila before he capped the bottle. He was feeling optimistic. He was proud of the new plan he'd developed on the fly. The idea excited him – the thought of him and his minions tearing through the open countryside, laying waste to anything in their path. He saw himself as Sherman cutting a swath across the American landscape or Napoleon rolling across Europe. He'd take what he wanted, when he wanted, where he wanted, how he wanted, just like he was doing here but with a lot less time and effort involved.

He nodded thoughtfully as he considered the future. Then he walked over to where the condo's front door stood open. The condo was empty and quiet now. "Just in case anyone is thinking about coming back," he said to himself as he reached inside his jacket pocket. He pulled a grenade from within, yanked the pin with his teeth, and tossed it into the condo's kitchen. Then he trotted down the staircase behind Ava.

* * *

The blast could be felt three floors below in the basement. Kate hugged the kids up close to her as dust and debris rained down from the ceiling upon the boxes that formed the roof of their tiny hovel. Violet let out a little squeal. Kate immediately covered the girl's mouth with a hand.

The three of them sat silently for the next several hours in the dark, cramped, dusty confines of the storage unit, terrified, listening for any sound of movement around or above them.

After the explosion, though, there was nothing…only silence.

Kate knew that if her husband, Chris, could get back to them, he would have. That either meant he was injured, he'd been taken prisoner, or…well, she didn't want to consider the last option.

There was a small window in the basement. Through the cracks between the boxes behind which they sheltered, she watched as the light faded outside until it was dark. It was then that she decided they'd waited long enough.

She rummaged through her pack until she found the flashlight and .38. Then she carefully and quietly moved the boxes around them until she'd created a tunnel large enough for her to exit their hiding spot. Before she left, she instructed Dylan that if she wasn't back in an hour, he was to care for his sister as best he could.

"Don't go, Mommy!" Violet whimpered. But her pleas did not deter her mother.

After Kate crawled from their small cave, she replaced the boxes so that her children remained concealed. Then she crept, without use of her flashlight, to the basement door. In one side of the door, there was a thin pane of wire-reinforced glass. She peered through this tiny window out into the blackness, trying to scan the darkened stairwell outside. She dared not turn the flashlight on to see. She feared that the people who had attacked

112

them earlier in the day might have decided to spend the night inside the building.

She cracked the door as quietly as she could, paused a moment to listen, then opened it carefully and slid out into the stairwell landing. There, she stood again, straining to listen. She detected the faint smell of smoke but heard nothing other than the occasional soft "pop-pop" of distant gunfire outside.

She made her way upstairs largely by feel, memory, and the faint ambient light the moon provided as it filtered through the stairwell landing windows. She paused every few steps to listen. Finally, she made it to the third floor where, in the moonlight, she could see the back door of their condo standing open.

She didn't want to go inside, but she knew she had to. She forced herself to step across the threshold.

The kitchen was a disaster, she could tell that even in the darkness. Years of living and cleaning a space bred a familiarity simply through feel and scent alone – a sixth sense of sorts.

Once inside, she flipped on her flashlight. The place was indeed devastated. She could barely walk through the debris and rubble that littered the floor.

She shined her light around the room. It illuminated charred cabinets, smashed countertops, a virtually non-existent sink, a melted microwave, a dented and blackened stove, and a floor covered in an array of broken dishware and crockery.

And then she saw her husband.

He was lying motionless on his stomach near where the kitchen met with the condo's central corridor. Kate's breath caught in her chest, her throat constricted, her stomach churned. She already knew, but she had to be sure.

She walked slowly, carefully, yet with forced determination through the debris strewn across the floor. Glass crunched under her feet. She kicked a spot near Chris clear and knelt beside him. Under her flashlight's beam, she could see that areas of his skin were blackened and his clothes had been burned away in spots.

It was a horrific sight.

Chris' head was turned so that she could see half his face. There were ashes and a few shards of glass on his cheek. She gently brushed them away. The lone eye she could see was closed. As she took his arm in her hand to feel for a pulse, she prayed that somehow he was still alive. But as her fingers touched his cold, stiff skin, she knew instantly that he wasn't.

She leaned over him to kiss the clean spot she'd revealed on his cheek. Then she sat back, resting her butt on her heels as she remained on her knees beside her fallen husband.

She sat staring at Chris, not wanting to absorb what she was seeing, but finding it impossible to tear herself away. She found it odd that no tears came until she tried to speak, and then they flowed freely.

"Thank you," she breathed softly, taking his cold hand in hers. "Thank you for everything…everything you've done, everything you did. I know my saying it now doesn't matter, but you saved us. You saved us in every way possible, right up until the very end. You saved us from the flu, saved us from starving to death, and saved us from the chaos that raged around us. You gave your life saving us, and it worked. You'll never know how much I love you, how much I owe you for that. And now it's our turn to save ourselves. Spending these past few weeks with you here, well…" she sniffled, wiping the tears from her cheeks with a hand, "…it made something horrible into something very special. You made a horrific situation into something that was almost tolerable. Without all the distractions of work, of television, of the internet and all the rest, I felt I grew closer to you and the kids than ever before. *You* made that possible. You were so strong for us. I only wish you could be with us now. But you never will be. You're gone…gone forever. You died to give us one more shot, and I promise that I'll do everything in my being to make your sacrifice worth it."

She held her dead husband's cold hand against her cheek. It felt odd, foreign, not like him.

At this point she broke down, unable to go on for several moments.

When she'd recovered, she choked out, "I love you…I've always loved you, and I *will* always love." Then she tore herself away, unable to bear anymore. This place was no longer her home, not without Chris. Now it was just a burned out space that held the remnants of what had once been their lives. But none of that mattered. She knew that Chris would tell her that the only thing that mattered now was the safety of the two children waiting for her downstairs. They were the only pieces that remained of her once vibrant and wonderful husband. And she vowed to do her everything in her power to ensure that those pieces remained safe from the hellish nightmare of the world in which they now had to survive.

At the back door, she paused, prepared to take one last look behind her...but she didn't. She didn't want to remember her once beautiful home this way. It was then that she noticed Chris' journal on what remained of the kitchen counter. She picked it up, brushed some ashes and other debris from its cover, and clicked off her flashlight. Then she stepped out onto the landing and moved forward slowly until she felt the stairway railing.

At the top of the stairs, something bumped against her leg. At first, she thought it was just more debris from their condo, but as she stood there, the object moved, rubbing against her. She was instantly frightened, but then made the connection. She stuck the .38 in her waistband, bent, and picked up the ball of fur that was Felix. She held him up close to her and he began to purr as she stroked his thick coat. It was a sliver of comfort in a terrible moment.

"I'm sorry," she rubbed his chin as he nuzzled his head down into her neck. "I completely forgot about you in all the commotion. Come on, the kids will be glad to see you."

She carefully made her way back downstairs to the basement carrying Felix with her. There, she quietly gathered the kids from their storage locker hiding spot. She surprised them with Felix, using him as a decoy to divert attention from the fact that their daddy was not with her. Then she made sure their packs were secured to them, that shoes were tied, and that the ground rules were explained and understood. While the kids were focused on petting Felix, she also took a few minutes to combine her pack of supplies into Chris' larger pack that they'd brought downstairs with them to await his arrival...an arrival that never came. The pack would be heavier and bulkier, but she knew that without her husband there to assist them, she'd need the additional supplies.

With everything set, she gave some final instructions. "No talking unless absolutely necessary," she reminded them. "You stick close to me unless I tell you otherwise. Dylan, I hold your hand, you hold your sister's hand. Got it?"

"Uh huh," he mumbled softly. "What about Dad? We can't leave him behind."

"He's going to meet us there," she lied. She didn't want to get into the issue of their father's passing right now. It would only slow them down and make things more difficult than they already were...for everyone. At the moment, she wasn't even sure if she could put into words what had happened to him. She was still processing it herself.

"Going to meet us *where?*" Dylan pushed.

It was a good question.

"West...we're heading west. We'll go out the back and cut up the alley to the train tracks. We'll start walking toward Aurora. We'll walk during the night and hide during the day until we get far enough away from the city's outskirts."

"How's Dad going to know where to find us," Dylan persisted innocently..

"I want Daddy!" Violet suddenly blurted out.

"*Shhhh...*" her mother hushed her. "He'll find us. But right now, we need to go. We're losing valuable travel time. I need you two to be strong and brave right now. Think of this as an exciting adventure...a night hike," she offered in her best attempt to make this horrible situation somehow appealing to the kids. It was something Chris was great at, and Kate smiled knowing that she was taking a page from his parenting playbook to get this done. He would have been proud of her – proud of all of them.

"*Oooo...*a *night* hike," Violet whispered.

Dylan remained silent. Kate wondered if he had already guessed what had happened to his father, but she dared not press him on it.

"Okay," she said, leading her children out of the basement and into the rear stairwell that exited to the alley, "we move fast until we're on the tracks. We don't stop for anyone or anything. Understand?"

"Yes," the kids both replied dutifully.

"What about Felix?" Violet asked. The cat had followed them to the back door and was rubbing against Violet's legs.

Kate took a deep breath, not really having considered what to do with their feline friend.

"We can't just leave him behind," Violet whimpered softly, picking the cat up and cradling him awkwardly in her arms.

"He can follow us," Kate said. "But if he can't keep up or strays during our hike, then he's on his own. He's a cat. He'll

116

have a better chance of surviving than…" she caught her self. "Well…he'll have a good chance of surviving. Cats are good at catching mice and stuff, remember?"

Violet and Dylan both nodded silently, and Violet let Felix slip as delicately as a four-year-old could down onto the floor.

Then Kate took a moment to pull Dylan close and kiss his cheek. He was getting so tall. The top of his head already came up to her shoulders, and it wouldn't be long before he matched her in height. Then she bent and lifted Violet. Her little girl clung to her, wrapping arms and legs around her tightly. Kate kissed her and squeezed her even more tightly to her.

"I'm kinda scared, Momma," Violet hissed in her ear.

"Don't be scared," Kate whispered back. "Just do as I say and we'll be alright."

With that, Kate let her slip back down.

"Everybody ready?" she asked.

"Yes," both the kids responded quietly.

"Everybody link up," she said, taking Dylan's hand in hers. She waited as Dylan got a good hold on Violet.

"Come on, Felix," Violet whispered as they moved toward the building's rear door. "You hang on tight to your sister," she told Dylan. "That's your only job right now; you hold onto me and your sister like you've never held onto anything before."

She reached out with the hand that she was also using to hold the .38 and cracked the door, listening for any signs of people outside. She heard nothing. Even the sound of gunfire had dissipated. Felix was with them, nose poked eagerly through the open crack in the door, sniffing the air.

Kate took a couple deep breaths and gave a slight wiggle to ensure her pack was secured snuggly to her. Then she said, "Ready…set…go!" and shoved the door open, leading all that remained of value from her former life into the terrifyingly new world that awaited them.

****

Be sure to get the next installment in the Pandemic Diary series – *Flee on Foot,* due out in May 2016!

****

Printed in Great Britain
by Amazon